"In these surgically-crafted stories Gary Wilson delivers bracingly honest and unsentimental portraits of ordinary people. The common theme is mortality. Facing it, avoiding it, causing it, even accepting it. A man chooses to ride out a hurricane to avoid his wife ("Camille"). A junkman entrepreneur fetches his alcoholic wife after an accident ("Going Home"). A barmaid mourns for a regular customer who nobody misses but her ("Small Talk"). A wife whose marriage has lost its spark, schemes to get rid of her husband ("For Those Who Favor Fire.")
Wilson has an artist's eye. His characters are vividly rendered with deft brushstrokes. He paints a picture of small-town Midwest America with clean, spare prose. An impressive collection."

—**Len Joy** is the award-winning author of *Everyone Dies Famous* and *American Past Time* among other works.

"In this intriguing collection, Wilson's sharply drawn characters, lonely as the bleak rural landscape that created them, are desperate to connect, whether they know it or not. They are presented with opportunities to do so, some as obvious as the need to deal with a newly discovered corpse, others as subtle as words that must be said in a fleeting instant. Will they act? Will they even notice they should? Written with brilliant economy, these unsettling stories will send a shudder down your spine and leave you with a desire to read everything else the author has to offer."

—**Rita Dragonette** is the author of T*he Fourteenth of September.* a coming of conscience story.

"Gary Wilson propels his short stories with quiet intensity in both his description and dialogue. Many of the stories in "For Those Who Favor Fire" use the geography of Kansas or another Midwestern setting, but each tale explores universal relationships among family or between strangers. These are not heroic or adventuresome tales, rather character reflections of people rooted in the land or just passing. Just as the renowned photographer Walker Evans captured images with his lens aimed at the stark truth of life in the Great Depression, Wilson's stories are both unadorned and revealing."

—**Timothy J. McNulty** recently retired from teaching at Northwestern University. He was also a correspondent and editor at the *Chicago Tribune* and co-author (with his son) of *The Meanest Man in Congress*, a biography of Jack Brooks, a Texan and 42-year veteran in the House of Representatives, published by NewSouth Books.

FOR THOSE WHO FAVOR FIRE

For Those Who Favor Fire

A collection of short stories

by

GARY D. WILSON

Adelaide Books
New York / Lisbon
2022

FOR THOSE WHO FAVOR FIRE

A collection of short stories

By Gary D. Wilson

Published by Adelaide Books, New York / Lisbon

adelaidebooks.org

Editor-in-Chief

Stevan V. Nikolic

For any information, please address Adelaide Books
at info@adelaidebooks.org

or write to:

Adelaide Books
244 Fifth Ave. Suite D27
New York, NY, 10001

ISBN: 978-1-956635-35-5

Printed in the United States of America

For
Modena
Christopher
and
Nicholas

Contents

Camille

He watches her watch TV with her singular intensity. Studies her, as though memorizing her looks against a time when she might not be here. The tilt of her head, darkening circles under her eyes, lines from her nose to the corner of her mouth, cheeks that sag more with each passing year. Hair brown, temple grey swept behind her ears and held with tortoise-shell combs that leave furrows where the teeth bite in. Green blouse with short sleeves and little red flowers that have black centers to match her black slacks and the black stripe on her white canvas shoes. Coordinated, together, ready to go.

Some people get religion. Millie got weather. Eighteen years ago they lost everything they had in a flood. Four years ago the same thing happened with Hurricane Betsy. She vowed then never to be caught flat footed again, and highs and lows, degree days, wind chill factors, frontal lines, radar images, rainfall records and such began to take on far more significance than mere figures on a screen would suggest. They became instead vital statistics, true matters of life and death to be noted, analyzed and acted upon accordingly.

As she's doing now, listening to the latest Lightning Bob Burk AcuWeather Update. A two by three feet piece of Masonite covers her lap. It has a map glued to it, a big one showing all of the Gulf of Mexico and the southern coast of the United States. A sheet of clear plastic has been taped over the top of it to keep it clean while she tracks storms, each in its own color—a series of red or blue or green circles with lines connecting them from start to finish, erasable at the end of the season. Camille is in black, a sinister parabola that cuts across the western tip of Cuba, turns and heads north. She's followed the storm from the very beginning, before it even had a name, when it was nothing more than a tropical disturbance, a mere depression, but one she nevertheless thought was worth keeping an eye on. And to hear it being described now—two hundred mile an hour winds, barometric pressure so low it's nearly off the scale, potentially the most dangerous storm of the season—seems to have filled her with an almost parental pride, as if Camille were her child, wild and unruly though she is, someone she alone understands well enough to predict the outcome of.

At least better than the National Hurricane Forecasting Center which still says Camille will follow the normal pattern, making landfall somewhere along the Florida Panhandle. She says they're full of it. She says the storm has a mind of its own and is heading straight for New Orleans. And when it hits, she says it'll make Betsy seem like a picnic.

"If you don't believe me, look for yourself," she calls out, even though he's no more than fifteen feet away in the kitchen where he's mixing the latest in a series of last drinks, stirring finger hanging limp over the rim of his glass. "There she is, not a single thing to stop her now from landing right smack dab on top of us, just like I said. I'm telling you, Sam, there's going to be at least five feet of water in here—maybe even ten. Could be that way over the whole city, as far as that's concerned. One tidal surge, one broken levee, that's all it would take, because there's no place for it to go. We're practically floating as it is, you know. It's the truth! Why else do you think they bury people on top of the ground here instead of underneath it like they're supposed to?"

A rhetorical question. As usual. She's on a roll, working up a real head of steam, and anything he might say about high water tables and their effect on local burial customs would definitely not be appreciated. You start thinking about one thing, after all, and it'll just lead to another and another. And who knows where you might end up then? Stuck somewhere not able to make a decision about anything, even when you have to. Even when it could mean the difference between dying and not. Like now.

She leans toward the TV, eyes wide, mouth open, like a woman gone blind or mad or both. She's never seemed so strange to him before, so ugly, and the thought of having to go anywhere, do anything with her fills him with dread. Especially getting into a car piled full of bags of this and that the way they have every summer since Betsy and driving and driving along with everyone else, as if they've all left at the same time on an ill planned vacation, forming a single unbroken line of lights outbound on Chef Menteur Highway, around the end of Lake Pontchartrain to points north. Like snakes swimming in droves out of the marshes whenever the water starts rising, up the canal, inland toward higher ground. Instinct. The urge to flee. The thrill of the chase. Of being chased. All of them seemingly stopping at the same filling stations and motels, OUT OF GAS/NO VACANCY signs popping up everywhere. Sleeping finally at a roadside park in northern Mississippi or Alabama, maybe even Tennessee, depending, and the next day limping back home, exhausted, the storm having by then been downgraded to a disturbance that did nothing more than spawn a few thunderstorms.

He has to look away. Wishes he could walk away. Takes a long drink instead.

"The way I figure it," she says, "We'll need to leave no later than tomorrow morning. Sooner if we want to be really safe and get a jump on the crowd. You remember how it was last year. So let's see, you get the suitcases from closet while I—"

"I'm not going anywhere," he says, a bit shocked at hearing the words aloud, as if a thought had slipped through before he could stop it. He's never opposed her before. At least not about the weather. Money and the weather.

She frowns, finger to her lips, head quivering slightly. "I'm sorry, I—"

"I'm staying here."

"Are you drunk?"

"Not in the least."

"That's how you sound."

"Sorry."

"You have had quite a few, even though I haven't been counting."

"Well I'm still not drunk."

"Okay, what is it then? What's wrong?"

"Nothing's wrong, Millie. Maybe I just don't see the reason for all the excitement. Maybe I think for about the tenth time you've blown the whole thing out of proportion and I'm tired of it and I'm not going anywhere."

"I see." A nervous little smile. "I'm just making this up? Is that the idea? As a way to torment you, make you more miserable than you already are? Good god, Sam, what's gotten into you? We're not talking about your run of the mill storm here. This one's a real killer. Everybody's saying so."

"Right. And they're also saying it's not going to hit anywhere near here."

"So? They have been known to be wrong once or twice, you know."

"And you haven't been?"

"Of course I have. I'm not saying that at all. But I've always thought it's better to be safe than sorry. And so have you."

"I have? How do you know that?"

"Sam, what on earth—"

"Did you ever ask me what I thought?"

"Some things don't need asking, do they?"

"Like what, Millie? Like whether you prefer apples to oranges? Whether you want your eggs sunny side up or turned over easy?"

"No," she says. "More like whether you want to live or die. Whether you still—"

"Still what?"

She shakes her head, tears in her eyes.

"Love you?" he says. "Love you enough? Something like that?"

"Something."

She waits.

He says nothing.

The sound of doors and drawers slamming in the bedroom eventually stops and he watches her lug two Pullman suitcases out and set them by the front door. She goes back for a cardboard box filled with books and pictures, a small metal file containing their personal papers, a pillowcase bulging with sheets and towels. She then unfolds a second, larger pillowcase and drags it around the kitchen and living room, taking whatever seems to catch her eye—a brass horse with a clock in its stomach, a framed needle point, their good silverware, a favorite teacup. With a final, impatient sweep of her arm, she clears the shelf behind the couch, keepsakes clanking and crashing all around her, and hefts the bag over to the door where she stands beside her goods, as haggard and forlorn looking as a refugee waiting for a train.

"I can't force you, Sam. I'm not big enough. And I don't have time to get you declared insane. But believe me, I thought about it, because you are crazy. You'd be a whole lot better off, you know, taking a gun and putting it to your head right now. At least then we'd know what was going to happen. At least then— Please, Sam? I'm begging you. I'll get down on my knees if it'll help. But please come with me. I am your wife, remember. We've been married thirty one years. That should count for something, I would think." She stiffens, glances away. "But whether it does or not is up to you. I'm going no matter what you decide. Right after I put these things in the car, I'm going."

Doors bang, the trunk lid whumps. There is a strange quiet between rushes of traffic on the highway, the night air heavy, full of smells—mud and salt and fish—full of presence, as palpable as warm dough, mosquitoes clinging like a second screen to the window.

Finished, she pauses, pale and trembling, in the doorway. "Well?"

He turns to look out the window above the sink. Is that it? That all? Well? What'd he expect? Hysteria? Screaming, crying, yelling? Being pounded on the chest, kicked in the shins? Cursed at? Called a rotten bastard? A dirty two-timing son of a bitch who never thinks about anything but himself and his goddamn job? Oh he could do a good one for her. Pull out all the stops. Give him enough to think about for the rest of his life, which according to her isn't going to be very long anyway.

But maybe she doesn't care that much anymore either. He never thought about that. Maybe well is the best she can do.

Except she did beg him to go, didn't she? Actually say she would get down on her knees? But that could have just been out of loyalty or something. Although he would like to know or at least ask now that his curiosity has been aroused.

"Wait."

The starter screeches. The engine roars through the open door.

He runs toward it, headlights flashing across him as she backs out of the parking pad onto the driveway.

"Millie!"

A squeak of tires on pavement and she's gone.

Midnight and Lightning Bob says everything's right on course. Camille is approximately 150 miles offshore, continuing to move slowly northward, winds remaining steady at or near two hundred miles an hour.

Sam marks the new coordinates on Millie's map, mentally projecting the path of the storm. If current readings persist, it should make landfall, as predicted, somewhere along the Florida Panhandle. Which could be worse, if it misses Pensacola and Panama City. A few palm trees get smashed, Camille dies quietly before reaching Gainesville or Jacksonville, and the worst, as Lightning Bob likes to say, is history.

Millie on the other hand. He picks up the road atlas lying next to him on the couch. He didn't get to ask her where she was going, of course, where she thought she might be. He didn't get to ask her anything. But if he were doing it, he'd go straight up Fifty nine toward Meridian, Mississippi. He doubts that she's much beyond Hattiesburg at this point. Maybe as far as Laurel, but that would be stretching it. Tired, looking for a place to stay over. A Holiday Inn, maybe. But she'd probably think that was too expensive, unless she was really mad. All you need's a place to sleep, she'd say. A clean bed and a TV. Motel 6 then. Red Roof Inn. He tries to think of a suitable place on that route but can't. All he can see is headlights on pavement, darkness all around, her driving that far by herself. Maybe having a wreck or a flat. He's isn't even sure she knows where the jack is. And who'd change the tire for her? That's another thing. And what about being a woman alone at a motel, checking in this late at night? Maybe if he hadn't been so damn stubborn. Maybe if she hadn't. Maybe then they could have sat down and talked it out, come to some conclusion. Found something to blame it on other than what they did. Or eventually will, if they haven't already.

Three o'clock in the kitchen, drink in hand—same or another he can't remember—staring out the window over the sink. Like looking into a fishbowl, images at first distinct, then blurred, oblique, and he can see himself peering back from the backdrop of the scene outside—rushes on the bank of the canal just beyond the trailer house bent to point inland by the wind, dark tops of trees above them boiling in the glow from the lights of New Orleans. And directly in the middle of the picture, on his forehead over each eye socket, a bright red dot flashing side to side, left right, left right from atop the main tower of the NASA installation three miles away at Michoud. Liftoff! We have a liftoff! The rocket inching up, holding steady, as if chained to the spot, as if dragging the earth with it like a giant ball, then breaking free into an arching white streak on the sky, gone, beyond sight, a dying match, the last pinpoint of light when you turn off the TV

Lightning Bob says Camille is a hundred twenty miles out and still on course. How would she look from up there? A certain beauty, he supposes, in the cloud formation. The grandeur of the swirl, the sweep, like a princess's gown at a royal ball seen from above. But going the wrong direction. Counterclockwise. A left handed princess.

Why hasn't she called? It's only common decency, after all. Put coins in the slot, dial the number. Even collect. Even from a bar, if she has to, although he wouldn't like that as well. Music, low voices, glasses tinkling. Maybe she looks better to somebody who's never seen her before. Doesn't know her. Hasn't lived with her—how long did she say? But she still could. Call and say hello. Nothing else—where she is, what she's doing—even if she doesn't want to. He would.

Six o'clock. Daylight, although it could be just another shade of night. Grey sky closing over grey land. A dreamscape, except he isn't asleep. Hasn't been yet and probably won't now that Camille's turned. Lightning Bob puts her a hundred miles out, but veering west. How far she'll come is anybody's guess, he says, since she's broken the rules and is more or less on her own, just as Millie predicted. Damn her if she's right.

He should eat something. Did they last night? He remembers Millie with—a bowl, was it? But not himself. Must have drunk his instead. A couple of leftovers of indeterminate age in the refrigerator. Some milk, a half carton of cottage cheese, a few slices of bread. Peanut butter. His stomach's so sour nothing sounds good, but he needs to. Has she? Is she now? He wonders if she has money. Her grocery envelope is still behind the canisters, the same fifty dollars in it she put there two days ago. Meaning she must have gone to the bank. No withdrawal slip in the drawer where she keeps them. So he won't know? Can't know? Was the whole thing planned? Even more than usual? Right down to his refusal to go? Did he play into it without realizing what was going on? Was that how she could say well? and be done with it? Because she knew she was going and not coming back?

Seven years ago they moved to New Orleans from Kansas for him to take a job with NASA, working on the Saturn V rocket engines that eventually sent the Apollo crew on the first leg of its flight to the moon. He couldn't have been more ecstatic. She couldn't have been more miserable, finding herself suddenly in a strange place with strange people who as often as not spoke an almost unintelligible language. She never really adjusted. Never made an attempt, outside of striking up friendships with a couple of women neighbors who were in the same situation she was. She might drink coffee with them once or twice a week, go to the Winn Dixie up the road, maybe to a department store occasionally. But that was it. The rest of the time she spent inside, watching TV, knitting, waiting like a prisoner day after endless day for him to walk in the door and tell her it was time to go back home. Which of course he never did, and which, he now realizes, may have been enough in the long run to push her over the brink. But still.

Nine o'clock. Seventy miles and closing. Like coming down a funnel, Chandeleur Islands at the mouth, mainland to the north, delta to the south, New Orleans at the tip. He thinks he hears the surf pounding but realizes it's the sound of his own heart.

By noon even Lightning Bob is gone. Camille is forty miles away, a force so brooding and ominous he has a sense that she could appear at the door at any moment and when he opened it, knock him stem winding. Goddamn her. You'd think she'd call, just to gloat if nothing else. To ask how he's doing, how he's feeling now. Tell him she wishes he were there.

The rains have come. Straight down at first, no wind. The final connection between earth and sky. Like the horizon in

Kansas. Like it must have been when the land there was covered by a great sea. Water everywhere. He can't remember ever having been so frightened.

And now the wind. Pressing, releasing, rain clawing the side of the trailer house, a sheet of corrugated metal shrieking as it rises, falls, rises on the roof of a paint shop at the rear of the property, empty black solvent drums stacked by the front door falling and rolling rumbling down the drive, off into the rising water from the canal. Trees sway like drunken giants, each gust stronger, longer. There are moments he can't take a breath.

Something's with him, which he can feel but not see, since the electricity's off and a grey haze covers all, making it dimmer yet inside. He cranes his neck to peer along the hallway, slowly, cautiously, expecting to find—what? Millie home to say she's sorry? Her ghost come to haunt him, to tell him it's his fault, because if he'd been with her she'd still be alive and so would he, alive together?

A great howling blast of wind and rain. The trailer house shudders, settles back, him with it, and there on the hallway floor, as flat against the baseboard as it can make itself, but still looking like a hose or a piece of black plastic pipe, is a five foot water moccasin, eyes glistening, tongue tasting the air. The wind moans. Snake's head raises toward him, mouth open, bright white, sun on snow white.

Easing himself onto the counter by the sink, he tucks his feet under him, lowers his head, hands over ears, squeezes his eyes shut and waits.

By evening it's over. What they get of it. The brunt of the storm, he hears on a transistor radio, hit near Gulfport, Mississippi. Pass Christian, to be exact, about sixty miles east of New Orleans. Damage is extensive, but no one's been able to get in yet to see just how bad things are. Maybe that's where the snake was going when Sam showed him the door, broom in hand. He slithered right over to it and out, barely a ripple where he slipped into the water, which as far as Sam could tell, hadn't risen above their top step. Traffic—a few cars and trucks—was still getting through on the highway. But otherwise it's quiet until the power comes back on and with it Lightning Bob saying how close it was and how lucky we are and in all honesty what a shame it is to live in a country that can put a man on the moon yet not do a better job predicting the weather.

He isn't sure how long she's been there when he wakes from a nap and finds her sitting on the couch like she's never been gone, looking just the same, only tireder.

"I was wrong," she says.

He rubs his eyes, blinks. She's still there. "Maybe so, but not by far."

"Split the difference with them, I guess."

"Yeah," he says. "Looks that way all right. So where'd you go?"

"Up the road."

"How far?"

"Couple hundred miles, give or take a few. Not much happening there. Lots of rain coming back though. Water's up almost everywhere."

"I'll bet. I've never seen anything like we had here. You stay over someplace?"

She nods.

"Where?"

"I don't know."

"Laurel? Meridian?"

"I was tired. I don't remember. Some motel somewhere up there. It had a bath and a bed and a TV so I could hear about the storm."

"Why didn't you call?"

"I don't know. Just didn't get around to it, I guess."

"What kept you so busy?"

"Driving. Thinking. I did a lot of thinking, Sam. Sleeping. But not so much of that."

"Me neither."

"I was awful scared. She could just as easily—"

"I know."

"They say it's real bad over around Pass Christian. Horrible. One place—an apartment building, big one—got completely destroyed. Smashed flat. Nothing left. Twenty three people killed there alone. Must have been something. Roads and bridges are out everywhere. Electricity. Lots of those big old houses on the shore took it hard, I guess, though I don't know if any of them are—you know—gone or anything. But I was wondering if maybe when things get settled here a little bit— tomorrow or the next day even—maybe we could take a ride over and see what the situation is for ourselves."

"Maybe."

"Well it's something to think about anyway. We can talk about it later."

Going Home

Her face feels mushy rotten from the inside. They are trying to save it, to firm it up again with gauze and stitches. She doesn't know whether they can. She doesn't care. A raw oyster of blood and mucus slides down her throat. Her stomach pitches. She closes her eyes, but they hurt, too.

She had a wreck and doesn't want to talk about it.

Rodney does.

"Vera, for the love of—"

In the side mirror, if she leans just right, she can see herself. Sunglasses cover eye slits, but there is nothing over the smashed nose, the bloated mouth, the cheeks that have taken on the sheen of burnished steel. They should have made her a mask. A skin one. From somebody's skin.

"I mean, you were drunk," he says.

Yes, she was.

"So drunk that two hours later you still couldn't walk straight."

Yes.

"And blind stumbling on your ass at three o'clock in the morning you decide to drive home."

That's what she was doing.

"Goddamnit, Vera, there were people in that car!"

The Cadillac surges, levels off. He resets the cruise control.

"Doesn't that mean anything to you?"

She sighs.

"You could've killed them."

The air conditioner sends her breath back. It tastes of rust. Like a junkyard smells. Oil-caked dirt, leaking batteries, stagnant water, moldy upholstery, rust. Like his junkyard, the one that made them rich. He won't call it a junkyard. It's a salvage lot.

On good days it's Pritchart's Automotive Recycling and Redistribution Center. She has watched him take visitors on guided tours. They arrive like moths, attracted by bright murals on the whitewashed fence. Waving his walking stick to and fro, he shows them through the gates. He halts. He pushes back his felt hat. He combs his fingers through grey thatch, as though deciding how best to proceed. He explains how he has set aside blocks of land for General Motors, Ford, Chrysler, American Motors and foreign products. Within each block the wrecks are further organized by make, model and year. He leads them past rows and rows of cars, along paths between the rows, down small streets between the big blocks where trucks can go in and out and a person can walk anywhere in the yard and know exactly where he is going. But no matter how excited Rodney gets about what he has done, no matter how enthusiastically he discusses it, the fact remains that he deals in junk.

Her tongue eases in and out of the space where her front teeth used to be. She practices the words before saying them.

"Where's my car, Rodney?"

He pushes his stiff leg to the floorboard. His body shifts. A bristled ear cocks toward her.

"My car. Where is it?"

The electric window opens. A gob of tobacco juice hangs in the air, shoots past.

"We got it. It's down by the old house."

She sees it there, a brilliant yellow sun next to the grey boards. The tow truck left it by the porch. It is parked at an odd angle, as though halfway down the drive she suddenly remembered something and hurried back to get it. The car is fine, except that the protruding V in front is now deeply inverted. The hollow headlight sockets are drawn in toward each other like blinded, crossed eyes.

"But I wouldn't worry about it if I was you," he says. "You won't be driving it or anything else for a good spell."

"That must make you happy."

"Don't see why it should," he says. "When you figure out what this damn deal's cost—"

"Because you've got me exactly where you want me."

"You're talking crazy, woman."

"I can't go anywhere now unless you take me. You or somebody."

"Who's that 'somebody'?" he says.

"There's the bus, I guess. I could take it. But that's not the same as being in your own car, going where you want to, doing what you want to do. I want my car back, Rodney."

"Your car you got," he says. "Your license you don't."

"It's not fair," she says.

He clamps his great hands over the steering wheel. "Fair? Fair, you say? Well just let me tell you a thing or two about fair. This isn't fair." He slaps his lame leg. "Neither's this." He thrusts his head to one side to show the scar running the length of his jawbone. "Nearly cost me my head. You know. You were there."

She was. Twenty-four years ago. It was the kind of evening when you would expect the phone to ring. Everything was too calm. The hot Kansas wind had died. Cicadas were screeching in the elms by the house. Mosquitoes were rising from the grass. The cat lay on top of the wringer washer on the porch. The dog drooped beside the steps where she was sitting. Rodney was off baling hay for Milo Rawlins. He was late, but that happened sometimes. The baler might have broken. They might be trying to finish a field in case of rain or to get up the windrows before dew settled on them.

She had learned to cook things that could wait to be served. The food didn't concern her. The phone ringing in her mind did. It meant something was wrong. He had been run into head-on by a half-ton truck less than a mile from home. They used a torch to cut him free from his car.

"I don't see any of that was fair," he says. "But it happened and instead of going around moaning and groaning I tried to make the best of it. I'd say I did a pretty damn good job, too."

She listened beside his hospital bed. Even there he was handsome. He was big and rugged, with dark skin browned by the sun. His eyes were so deeply black they appeared as wide holes opening into his soul. And she loved to hear him talk. His voice was firm and resonant. Like a preacher's the way it carried right through her, excited her.

He was going to turn misfortune into fortune. He explained that running a salvage lot was like being an undertaker—both disposed of things nobody else knew what to do with. When you did it right, you made a profit. But an undertaker made a profit only once. A salvage man—even then he wouldn't say junk—could make a profit over and over until there was nothing left of the car. Every wreck was a gold mine in parts.

Some mornings that summer she would awaken and find him propped against pillows. A cigarette would be suspended between his thumb and index finger an inch or so from his lips. He would be gazing off, smiling as though he were reading a joke someone had written on the far wall. When he noticed that she was looking at him, he would stub out the cigarette and roll over to stroke her bare back and to tell her all that they were going to have and see and do.

But the salvage lot seemed more than dreamy talk. He told her it would make them rich. She didn't doubt him. Paul Olfield's insurance company was already willing to pay Rodney's medical bills and even some extra for his leg. Bill Winkler, their lawyer, told them the insurance people would chip in another good chunk since Olfield was so far in the wrong, barreling down the road like something was after him, and on Rodney's side to boot. Bill said all Rodney needed to do was mention lawsuit and they'd come around fast enough.

"You're going to junk it, aren't you?" she says.

He glances in her direction. That is all he has done for days. He never fully meets her eye. Not that he could. Not that she cares.

"Haven't decided yet," he says.

"Is it totaled?"

"No, but there's no way to drive it and no way to sell it in that condition without taking a beating. Can't afford to fix it, either, just now. May never be able to when they're finished with us."

"Couldn't you set it way out back and let the weeds cover it up?"

"Bury it?"

"Sort of," she nods.

"But you don't want to see it go piece by piece, right? A generator here, a tire there. The wheel covers are a big item. They move fast. We could parcel it out the way we got rid of the furniture from the old house. Sure, we'd save a thing or two back—maybe a headlight rim or the steering wheel. We'd put them up on the wall in the family room, right next to the divan and chair you kept. Just to remind us, I think you said."

"Why are you—"

"Goddamnit, Vera!"

He swore then, too, and slapped his walking stick into the wall outside her hospital room. Bill Winkler had just told him that the people she'd run into were suing for a million and a half. She was supposed to be asleep, but she heard everything.

"There's only one possibility, my friend," Bill said. "Since she was so drunk, you can't throw yourself on the mercy of the court. Not with that bag of flint Parsons up there. But what you can do is tell him Vera's been acting odd for a long time. She's been under a lot of strain. She hasn't been well—you know—mentally. It'd be worth a bundle, if he bites. And it wouldn't be entirely untrue, would it? Really? I mean, what the hell's been going on, Rodney?"

His cheek bulges, as though a thought is stuck there.

"I built you a new house, didn't I?" he says.

Swirling fields of wheat roll by. Dusky hedgerows divide plots, break the wind. A hawk tilts and soars. Far down the shimmering tracks that parallel the highway a light rotates in and out of view as a train approaches silently.

"Didn't I?" he says, swallowing instead of spitting.

She clears her throat. She nearly gags on what she dredges up. She hates him.

"Yes," she says softly.

"And I bought you clothes?"

"Yes."

"And jewelry?"

"Yes."

"And made sure you always had enough money?"

"Yes."

"And didn't I buy you that car? That very same car?"

"Yes," she says. "But—"

"But what? Come on. Out with it."

The train is upon them. The blaring horn fades like a dream.

"I'll tell you then. There's not going to be any more, that's what." Dark triangles of tobacco have lodged between his bottom teeth. "They want a million and a half dollars we don't have. We're broke, we're bankrupt, we're on our way to the poor farm. Why, we'll end up worse off than we were twenty-five years ago."

She shuts her eyes to the rush of boxcars. "Maybe—"

"You're thinking maybe that wouldn't be so bad, right?" he says. "Maybe if we could just step back there to the good old days everything'd be hunky-dory."

"Maybe it would have been better if—"

"Back there when we didn't know for sure where the next can of beans was coming from. Back there when we didn't have a damn thing of our own free and clear. Those the good old days you're thinking about? Moon all you want, then. Tell me how wonderful they were. Tell me how much better it was when I spent all day shoveling somebody's shit or cutting their hogs. Tell me—"

A trainman pokes his head out the window of the caboose. She raises her hand to wave, checks herself. The trainman glances down, sunglasses glinting, and passes on.

"Better if what?" Rodney asks suddenly, as though he's only just heard what she's been saying.

"Maybe it would have been better if I had killed them."

"You gone plain mad, woman?"

"It wouldn't have cost you so much. I heard Bill Winkler say it was a straight ten or fifteen thousand for each one."

"Vera? Vera, listen to me."

"Or if anybody was killed it should have been me. That would have made it easier for you with the judge."

The car slows. "You keep talking that way and we're going back. We'll get you another doctor. A head doctor. One of those shrinks. That's what you need, sure enough. You need somebody to let down that swelling. To get the bloat off."

"Like a cow that strayed into the wrong pasture?"

"Like a cow." He stares straight ahead, guiding the car with two fingers laid loosely over the crossbar of the steering wheel. His lips twitch. She can't tell whether it was going to be a smile or a frown.

He had the same look the afternoon he woke her from a nap and led her to the bedroom window of the old house. Far at the south end of the salvage lot his restored Plymouth had been raised on a thirty-foot platform. PRITCHART'S was spelled out in big white letters the length of the car. She glanced at him. Despite herself, she snickered. A corner of his mouth drew up. She laughed. He stepped back. "Oh, Rodney," she gasped. He broke, sputtering, roaring, like a stubborn engine coming to life.

That was long ago. It was before they removed the bed and other furniture, taking what was left with them to the new house.

A rock whacks the underside of the fender. She jerks alert. Her heart pounds in her temples, in her sinuses, in every cut and bruise. A gravel road stretches like a chalk line ahead of them. In their wake, white braids of dust boil up to form a thick cloud that spreads slowly away on either side of the road, down over hedge trees and scrub oak, ditch weeds.

He is driving the back way home.

It is the back road into Bartlett's Junction. At the west edge of the city park it becomes paved, swings sharply toward the towering Co-op elevator and the long, squat Butler building that smells of tear gas after each harvest. It leads straight then to the center of town. There is a stop sign between the bank and a drug store. A left turn onto Main Street, past the coin-operated laundry, the grocery store, block after block of approaching cars and pickups, people out for afternoon strolls, people in their yards looking on. Everyone looking on.

"Why are you going this way?" she says.

"It's shorter. It's different. Haven't come along here in quite a spell." He shrugs. "No particular reason, I guess."

"Why don't you just tie my hands and walk me in behind the car? That's the way outlaws used to be brought in."

"Now there you go again," he says.

"That's what I am, isn't it? Your prisoner?" A trickle of blood oozes down her throat. "Parade me before the people. Show them what you've gotten for your efforts."

His right eyebrow arches. He seems amused.

"Your pay-off, your reward," she says matter of factly. Her head dips. She hisses. "Why are you doing this to me, Rodney?"

"Well, I suppose you could say—"

"Damn you! God-damn you! I will not be humiliated like this! I will not be led around in front of my friends like your little puppy dog!" An arrowhead of pain surfaces between her eyes.

He rolls his head toward her.

"You've got it all wrong," he says finally. "It's nothing like that. Why, I'm doing you a favor. I'm giving you one last chance to show your stuff, Vera."

"You son of a bitch!"

"Isn't that what you were doing in Wichita? Showing your stuff?"

"I told you I was—"

"Riding around. That's what you said. Riding around showing your stuff."

"No, that isn't—"

"At three o'clock in the morning. Drunk. You get drunk riding around?

Oh, no, there were bars. You told me there were bars. Where you talked to people. You like to talk to people, you said. That all you like?"

"I hate you."

"Kind of lonely riding around like that, isn't it? It's nice to have some company. You pick up one of those chatty boys at a bar?"

"I hate every bone in your body."

"And you and him ride around, maybe sipping a little now and then? Still showing your stuff, for sure. Could be you showed your stuff to each other."

"There wasn't anyone."

"Did he like your stuff? You like his?"

"Rodney, please. For the love of god."

"Why, what better fun could there be? Riding around like that on the broad avenues of Wichita, getting drunk, showing—"

"Nobody was there!"

"Don't lie to me! I read the police report. A witness said he saw somebody—a man—leaving your car at the time of the accident. Deny that! Go on, deny it!"

"I don't—"

"Was he driving?"

"I'm trying to tell you—"

"Was he?" His breath stinks. "The truth, goddamnit! Was he driving!"

"There wasn't anybody!"

The brakes jam on. The car slides sideways in the road. Gravel shoots into the air and falls against the windows and onto the hood.

"Whore!"

She ducks. The back of his hand rakes the top of her cheek and grazes her forehead. His open palm twists her head back. The brief, sharp pain plunks to nausea.

She peers with some curiosity at the blood spatters on the window.

"Tell me he was driving, you slut!"

His walking stick. She doesn't dare forget about it. She finds the release button for the seat belt. She frees herself. She opens her door.

"Why are you protecting him?" he calls after her. She walks farther away. "Is he worth everything we have? Everything we've ever had?"

"I've said all I'm going to say." She holds a kleenex to her nose. "I'll walk from here, thank you."

A massive solid glob sticks in her throat. She goes to her knees, arches her neck, opens her mouth, like someone before an executioner. Blood and mucus and rice gush out. A fountain. A fountain with grey-green monsters lurking at the edge. She smells fresh air, bites it, swallows it. Rancid cabbage. She hunches forward, catching herself with her arms. "Dear God, please, Dear God, let me die. Let me die."

She comes to in the car. They are parked in the driveway of their home. She gropes for her sunglasses to cut the glare from the white siding.

Neither of them talks, neither of them makes a move to get out. They will have to soon because of the heat.

Gary D. Wilson

What You Don't Know

She says she's not going to live forever and before she dies there's something she wants to tell me, something nobody else on earth knows about, but that I should. How soon can I be there?

The sun hasn't risen yet, but I get out of bed and shower and shave. It's perfectly clear what I have to do.

The click of a handle on the chest of drawers brings my wife up, suddenly awake, covers clutched to her throat.

"David?"

I smile, hoping to reassure her.

"What are you doing?"

"Getting dressed."

"I can see that. Why are you getting dressed?"

"I have to get to the airport."

"I didn't know you had a trip scheduled."

"I don't. Not for work."

"For what then?" She's suspicious but hasn't decided why yet.

I finish tying my shoes and check to see that I have my bank card. I'll need cash.

"David? You have to tell me where you're going!"

"I'm going to see Aunt Hattie."

"Oh, David!"

"She wants to talk to me."

"How do you know?"

"She told me."

"When?"

"I have to go."

"No you don't." The covers drop as she reaches out to me.

I sit on the edge of the bed and take her hand and try to explain one more time. "I want to get it over with, Alice. I want to be able to sleep again."

"You don't really believe that's what's happening, do you?" she says. "That since she doesn't have a phone she talks to you in your dreams?"

"I don't know. I mean, maybe. Somebody does."

She flops back against the pillow, exasperated. Won't look at me now.

"I owe it to her, Alice. What can it hurt if I go and hear her out and it relieves her mind and she can die in peace? What's so bad about that? Alice?"

She glances at the ceiling, the bookcase, eyes moving quickly over the titles. "It doesn't make any difference what I say—or don't—does it? You'll go no matter what. You've already made up your mind."

"I don't have a choice."

"Of course you do."

I shake my head. "Not in this."

"And what about work? You do have a job, you know."

"Call them for me and tell them I'm sick." I smile at my own joke. She doesn't. She wouldn't smile if her life depended on it. And I don't blame her, I really don't. I lean over the bed to kiss her and get a mouthful of hair.

"Please try to understand."

I wish I did. I wish I could tell for sure if it were a dream. I wish I knew beyond a doubt that standing in line to buy a plane ticket at O'Hare is real and Aunt Hattie talking to me is not. But I don't.

She really isn't my aunt, although that's what I've always called her. She's my great aunt. Hattie Barlow. Mad Hattie, some of the kids used to say. I haven't seen her to speak of since I was a kid myself—that's part of the problem for Alice; she can't figure out why it's so urgent for me to visit someone I haven't been around for thirty years—and then only at big family gatherings where she usually sat off to one side alone. People would go over, say a few words and move on. She was considered too unpredictable to risk long involvement. She might suddenly shout or laugh or say something outrageous. To those who didn't know her, she was described, in a whisper, as being "a little different, you know. Not quite right, poor thing." I didn't know whether she was crazy or not. I was just a kid. I couldn't judge a thing like that. I only know how old she seemed. Ageless, bent, with a musty odor children naturally shy away from. I rarely had anything to do with her beyond an obligatory hello or fetching something my mother or father told me to take her. When I approached her on those occasions, she would grasp my offering in one bony hand and trap my arm with the other, holding on with a grip that neared pain. I would try to make the best of it, smiling and nodding as she said thank you and I said you're welcome, not looking any longer than I had to at those piercing gold brown eyes. They were scary for a kid.

And they've been there every night for a week. Just at the edge of consciousness where everything is clearest. Two pinpoints of pure energy. And her hand squeezing my arm, a touch so vivid I wake searching for marks on my skin, the bed wet with sweat, sheets torn loose and tangled, Alice wide eyed, asking questions beside me. And the message is always the same.

The plane is nearly full and strangely quiet. Everyone but me is dressed in a suit. Even the women. And they're all reading—contracts, the Wall Street Journal, proposals and counterproposals, USA Today. I came unprepared. I have nothing but an Ambassador magazine I've read twice already. I lean back and close my eyes.

The plane taxis to the runway. We turn. Bells chime. The thrust of the engines pushes me back in my seat, giving me substance.

A hundred years ago a wagon train traveled roughly the same route we fly. A small group, seven families, all going from the prairies of Illinois to the prairies of Kansas. New land, new hope. The journey is difficult, but it takes on a certain rhythm. Daylight to dark, regardless of the weather, peering down a dirt track cut by countless other groups like our own. Today I ride in the wagon. A girl with brown braids leans against my shoulder. Sarah. My/his sister. I can see the straight pale part down the center of her head, hair pulled back on either side like stitches in coarse cloth. I can hear the clang of pots above us as the wagon sways, the creak of leather harnesses, the low rumble of wooden wheels turning on packed earth. I can smell the sweat of oxen, wood smoke lingering in the canvas covering the wagon. A boy walks beside us, a bit ahead, actually, to avoid as much dust as possible. My/his brother Thomas. He wears overalls, a blue shirt and a floppy felt hat. No shoes. Yet he seems oblivious to stones and prickly grass as he fairly floats along, his gaze fixed on something ahead of us, as if he's in a trance. And the voices I can just make out must be his parents'. But I can't tell. Why am I so cold? I put my arms around the girl and curl up close to her. She doesn't move. Why do I feel so alone? Suddenly I want to stand up and shout, tell them it's all right, but I can't because it isn't and won't ever be and somehow it's my fault that they're all dead. It's a dead wagon I'm on and the voices are coming from behind instead of in front and are not familiar at all, and my/his parents are wrapped in sheets on the floorboard, along with my/his brother and sister, and the boy beside the wagon is gone now and the girl I'm holding is really a doll.

I sit up and watch our final approach to the Kansas City airport. We descend lower and lower toward brilliant green fields and trees, and I have the unnerving impression, without knowing why exactly, that what I have just experienced was not so much a recollection as a rehearsal.

I rent a car with no trouble. It's a pleasant drive over the rolling hills of southeast Kansas. Old familiar territory. Olathe, Ottawa, Garnett, and at last, Colony.

An asphalt road curves off the main highway and leads toward railroad tracks that are weedy and rusted from disuse. Across them is the town, a single block of businesses—grocery, hardware store, bar and furniture and appliance dealership on one side of the street, Co-op elevator and Post Office on the other. The storefronts are dim, displays faded a uniform grey by the sun. Rusty pickups, some with side racks, some without, angle in toward the curb. A lone farmer tugging at the bill of his John Deere cap watches my car go by, his eyes coming to rest, as always, on the license plate.

At the end of the block, brick gives way to gravel. Dust rises behind me, drifting over lawns and bushes and the ubiquitous squat, white frame, apparently foundationless dwellings that line the streets.

Aunt Hattie's is the last house on the south side of town. It is the Dawes family house that her father built at the beginning of the century and is one of the only two or three in Colony that has any size or dignity. She came by it simply by outliving everyone else, and as she waits for me at the top of the steps, perhaps a bit put out that it's taken me so long to get there, she and it seem to fit hand in glove, both tilting slightly north, as if they too are gradually, and almost without notice, succumbing to time and the wind.

She seems even smaller than I remember. Not an inch over five feet, and then only if she could straighten up, which I doubt she can. She's wearing a long black skirt over black high-top shoes and what looks like a man's castoff cardigan under a dark blue crocheted shawl. Her hair is in a tight knot on top of her head, white wisps going off this way and that like curls of smoke. She's toothless now, her face sunken as a rotting jack o lantern, skin so wrinkled it seems nearly smooth again. Witch comes to mind. A cousin called her that once and I remember being embarrassed, hoping she hadn't heard, as I'm hoping she hasn't read my thoughts now, since part of me is convinced she can just by turning those eyes in my direction. They haven't changed at all.

She has coffee ready and we sit on the porch to drink it. It's a nice late spring morning with sunshine and bird songs and the sweet smell of irises and alfalfa. There is a breeze though, as there always is in that country, and despite her wrap, she seems chilled. I suggest that we move inside, but she won't hear of it, and as we talk, the chill seems to come and go. I even feel it a time or two myself. Or at least I think I do.

She's going on ninety-five, she says, and with the natural impatience old people sometimes develop out of fear that they may not live to tell their tales, she quickly dispenses with the niceties—how was my trip/how is my wife/how is my job—and plunges directly into the heart of the matter.

"You're the last Dawes. The last one to carry the name. My father, your great-grandpa, Old Man Marcellus, they called him, he had three sons. And me, but I don't count. Not in this. Now only two of the boys married and just one had children. That was your Grandpa Pete. He had two sons. One of them died young. You never knew him. So that left your daddy, Bill Dawes, and he only had you. And you don't have any. Won't either at your age. So the way I figure it, that makes you the end of the line. And that's why I called you here. There's only me and you left. Everybody else, they're dead and gone." She tilts her head toward the cemetery, visible across a field to the south, the sexton's shed in the center, family markers rising and falling in an irregular pattern against a backdrop of swaying poplars. "And I will be soon enough myself. Every day I think this is it, my time's come. But then I eat and sleep and get up all over again. And here I am, still here. Not worth much though. Why I've seen better looking corpses than me. Can't trust my legs a minute, and my hands, why I can't remember the last time I got a lid off a jar by myself. And there's my back. Look at that."

She turns her hump toward me. I nod in appreciation of her problem and hope she won't ask me to touch it.

"No, the only thing left working on me is my mouth and my brain. My mouth, it only gets me in trouble. Oh I know what they say about me, no use denying it. I've heard them, times when they figured I was sleeping or too far out of it crazy to know. But you've got to be careful about that, thinking somebody's crazy when they're not. Real careful. I for one have never been crazy a minute in my life. I don't care what they say, I always know what's going on—and then some. Why right now my brain's clear as a bell. It's not supposed to be, I know, but it is. My brain's fine, healthy as the day I was born. And you know why? Because it's thinking all the time. Thinking and thinking and thinking. About them," a flick of the eyes toward the cemetery, "and us and what it means."

I shift in my chair to throw off the chill as she hunkers down in hers, one eye squinted shut, her mouth, her whole face puckering like the end of a drawstring bag. Then it slowly relaxes, her other eye opening and both together fixing on me as she leans forward, hand deep inside the cardigan, face worried, relieved, worried again, like someone trying to find the source of an itch. She straightens finally and withdraws her hand, in it a picture, a brown and faded sepia print with water marks along the right border, which she stands against the cream pitcher on the table between us.

"You ever seen this one, this here picture?"

I shake my head.

"That's him. My pa. Your great grandpa, Marcellus Dawes. I don't know for sure when it's from, and it's not the best one of him, but you can still get the idea."

He's standing alone, his right hand grasping the lapel of his heavy, dark coat, his left arm cocked behind his back. A watch fob stretches across the front of his vest, and he has a stickpin and the starched collar of the period, its points folded neatly down on either side of the knot of his tie. He's a tall man with a lean, angular face framed in a full dark beard. He is not smiling.

"See? See? You're wondering why he isn't, too, aren't you?" she asks, as though she has indeed read my thoughts. But I have no chance to answer before she delcares: "Guilt. Unbearable guilt," like a judge pronouncing sentence on a doomed man.

I look again at the picture. Closely. At the eyes. What kind of guilt am I supposed to see? That of a womanizer? A gambler? A drunk? Or maybe a man so aloof and distant he was incapable of loving? What? Because I see no guilt at all, not a hint as he stares steadily at the camera, and through it, into the future. There is no embarrassment, no remorse, no indication that if he could live his life again he would change a single thing.

I look back at her.

"I suppose just like me you were raised to believe everything you heard about him—how he started out here on that wagon train from Illinois and on the way everybody in his family except him died and that that childless but well to do couple, the Daweses, took him in and brought him on to Kansas and adopted him as their own. And how, despite all his bad luck, he didn't give up. How he just lowered his shoulder and went right into it and made good. So good he married the banker's daughter and rose to be a first class citizen. So good you're still reaping the benefits of his hard work. That story? And I'll bet just like me, you were raised to think that what you don't know can't hurt you. Right? Wrong. All that does is delays things. What you don't know's still there. It's still there and it's going to come round sure as anything. You're going to find out one way or another, sooner or later. You have to, you see, because the circle's not complete till you do. Till it's passed on. Nobody can rest proper till then. Not him, not me, not your grandpa or your daddy. I don't know about you, what you'll do. You've got nobody to tell like I have. Except maybe for your wife. Except maybe for her."

I'm listening. That's what I came to do. I promised. But I don't have to say anything. I don't have to agree or disagree, and I don't have to look at her. I try not to, my eyes fighting hers not to be drawn in, only to listen and be done with it, to listen so she can die in peace and I can go home and not think about her any more. And sleep.

"That night before he died—my pa, your great grandpa—he sent for a priest. Said he wanted to confess, which took us all by surprise, since he wasn't really what you'd call a religious man, let alone a Catholic. On the outside, sure, on the side he showed people. He was a businessman, after all. But not on the inside. He never prayed once that I know of, and the only time he ever said God's name was in vain. But he wanted that priest. I know it for a fact. I was there. Problem was we didn't have any priests in Colony, never have had, so we had to send down to Iola for one. Came as soon as he could and went into the bedroom and shooed everybody else out. Me included, but I stayed right by that door. Didn't move an inch. And I was still there when the priest came out. He was a young man, I remember, and he tried to smile and show us everything was all right. Which it couldn't have been, not with him that pale and shaken. Everybody else thought it was because he was young and didn't have a lot of experience with dying and all. But I knew different. As soon as he reached down and touched me on the head, I knew. I can still feel it. I can still feel his fingers trembling there as he said, 'Bless you, my child.' Just like that. 'Bless you.' And something happened. Like a shock, only warm, and it went all down me and back up and stuck in my brain. And I realized then it was something special, a special knowledge he was giving me. Just by laying his hand on my head like that he could pass it on to me without saying a word. He could let me know what went on in there, what my pa told him in that dark room. Just like I'm going to tell you now. Only I have to use words because I don't have the power that priest did."

"Like hell," I say, suddenly recalling the vision I had on the plane.

Her eyes narrow, locking on me. It's painless. I don't feel a thing but the sensation of energy, of emotion, of time rushing out, much as it does just at the moment of sleep.

She's telling me he murdered them. Poisoned them, so they died in their beds. That's what you can see in his eyes. That's why he can't smile. He doesn't dare. There's blood on his teeth. Blood on his hands. Blood on all our hands. And it won't wash off. And I can hear you saying how could he do it? How could a ten year old boy do such a thing by himself? He didn't. They helped him. They put him up to it, them whose name he came to have. Dawes. They wanted him and took him, and he became theirs. Him and his black deed that he lived with all his life, until at the moment of dying he couldn't stand it anymore and called for the priest and passed it on to him and him on to me and me on to you, and now it's yours and I'm finished.

Her head drops to her chest, her eyes close. She breathes evenly and is soon snoring.

"Aunt Hattie?"

I touch her shoulder.

"Aunt Hattie!"

"Humph!" She looks up, blinking. "What is it? What's wrong? Oh. It's you. I was just resting my eyes. But maybe I better go on in. It's getting cool again and I'm tired. That is, if there wasn't something else you wanted."

The plains are more reassuring from the air than from the ground. At thirty-five thousand feet, you can see outlines of rivers and farms, roads and towns. Their patterns make sense. The idea of westward expansion seems reasonable, that people would want to come settle here, to live here and raise their families, and to die here, generation after generation. But on the ground, it's more difficult to maintain such a clear perspective, where there is only the sky and the land and the horizon and a single day, sunup to sundown, can last forever.

It's well after midnight when I get home. Alice is in bed, asleep. I undress in the dark, put Marcellus Dawes' picture on the chest of drawers and lie down beside her.

She rouses enough to touch me, make sure I am who she thinks I am, mutters "I love you," then settles back down.

I have to decide. If I say anything at all, she'll want to know everything that went on, and if I tell her I'm not sure, it'll only make her feel worse. Make her angry, afraid, worried she's losing me—or already has—to something that doesn't make sense, that isn't explainable. And maybe that's the problem. Maybe it all falls apart when you start talking about it. Sounds trite, silly, crazy even. Maybe you have to have the power the priest had, Aunt Hattie has. Maybe if I just reach out and touch Alice on the head— But once you start, there's no turning back. Once it's over, she'll be the one who knows. She'll be the end of the line, like I am now. And what will she do? How will she ever sleep again?

Moonlight casts shadows of branches on the wall, leaf buds at their tips beginning to unfurl. And I think what a good idea, what a great idea. Sleep. The shadows grow an inch, then two, then three. A hell of an idea. I glance at the east window, wondering how long it will be.

The Auction

Orin stood gazing across the narrow beachhead of lawn that separated his house from the old woman's. The odor of fried sausage cakes and Dewberry's uncleaned pipe lingered in the menisci of fog lining the corners of the kitchen window.

"I just think it's too bad," Dewberry said, pushing back his red cap and scratching his shock of white hair. "Kind of sad in a way."

"Not a damn thing sad about it. She had her chance—several times."

Dewberry knocked pipe ashes into his saucer, his bad eye, milky and unfocused, peering up at Orin, who always had an impulse to put the eye back in place or cover it or make Dewberry turn his head. "Now what chance does an old woman have?" he said, pipe set again in his teeth.

"More than you and me, I'll tell you for sure," Orin boomed, face reddening. "Do you know that women—widows—control seventy-five per cent of the money in this country? Figure that out and tell me about chances."

"It don't do you no good if you ain't got nothing else." Dewberry banged his cup on the table. "Give me some more coffee."

"There's the pot." Orin's finger shook with an old man's palsy.

"Some restaurant you run." Holding the counter to keep his balance, Dewberry splattered coffee into his cup. "All I'm saying is the old woman was alone and didn't have no choice. To me that's a sad state."

"You're a crying old flea bag then."

Dewberry nursed the full cup back to the table.

"Nobody forced her and her old man to live like they did," Orin went on. "You buy the biggest house in town and shut yourself up in it and let everybody else go to hell, you can't expect much more. They didn't have no friends, even when he was alive. Too good for everybody, I guess. That kind of sadness you bring on yourself. You can't live sealed up in a mausoleum. You have to keep your friends. Work at it."

"That's true enough," Dewberry nodded, stirring the thick coffee.

"And by God I've worked at keeping my friends all my life. Even on the railroad there was never a man said a thing against me. That's a mark when you're foreman."

"Imagine so," Dewberry slurped.

"Far as that old lady's concerned, I tried. Damned if I didn't. She finally let me mow for her. Nothing else, though. Wanted to plant some new bushes on the north side there where they put in the new water line." He jerked his thumb toward the house. "I thought some greenery'd cover up that old siding. Looks like it's got fungus, hasn't been painted in so long. She wouldn't have nothing to do with it. Didn't do no good to talk. Same thing when I wanted to fix the door on her screen porch. Too damn independent. Didn't want to lean on nobody."

"Suppose there's some truth in that." Dewberry twisted the point of a carefully rolled napkin into his ear.

"You know there is. You get too big and mighty and there's nobody but yourself to blame. She just got where she couldn't do nothing herself." He rubbed the grime on the window, spiraling the autumn sun through the spot. "No, Dew, she's best off in that home she went to. Toward the end she took to staying in one room. Right on the corner next to me. The only place lit up at night. Rest of the house was dark as hell. Spooky."

"I know. I seen it, too." He held the napkin to his good eye, then dropped in on the table.

"I was in there once to get my mowing pay. Thought I'd never get to where she was calling from. Must have gone through four or five rooms, all dim and damp with the shades down and all the furniture covered up with sheets. Felt like the place'd been closed up for years." He swiveled his shoulders at the chill.

"You get a good look at any of the stuff she had?" Dewberry grimaced as he worked on his ear with a matchstick.

"Only what was in her room. It all looked pretty moldy, dirty."

"Just wondering, cause I heard there was some good stuff left and that antique dealers was going to be crawling around here like termites. Bids'll start high, you can bet, so high nobody else'll be able to buy nothing."

Dewberry struck the match and lit his pipe. "You going over?"

"Maybe for a while later." He stepped back from the window and cocked his head. The auctioneer's assistants had just set a table near the dwarf maple he had planted. As they snapped up the leaves, each caught a piece of the sun on its burnished surface, spinning the light in its grain and working it into sweet, dark honey. "Maybe I'll go over. There could be a thing or two, you can't never tell."

"What'er you looking at? You got your mind set on something already?" Dewberry stood beside Orin, squinting his good eye, while the other stared crazily at the ceiling.

Orin was tempted to look up but went for coffee instead. "I don't have my mind set on nothing." He knew Dewberry couldn't make out anything beyond the edge of his lawn, so he wasn't worried that he would see the table. "Just thought it might be interesting to go over and find out what the old woman really did have now it's uncovered and out in the open."

"Your jaw was twitching. Never does unless you got your mind set." Dewberry turned, wiping the corners of his mouth on his wrist, as he did when he was too excited to swallow. "What is it?"

"I'm telling you it's nothing." His hand trembled as he unplugged the coffee pot. "All I got my mind set on is wrapping pears."

Dewberry's roving eye moved into concert with the other. When both eyes focused on him, Orin sensed that Dewberry could see inside his head, like a television screen, could see him in the old woman's house when he had spied the table leg—just an inch or two of it—sticking out under the sheet and him going over to hike up the sheet, lifting it slowly up the smooth leg and the old woman hearing him and calling out because she thought he had gone and him standing there dumbly running his callused hand over the waxy skin of the table trying to keep from breathing too loud and now him lying to Dewberry for the first time about anything important, shutting him out because he was afraid Dewberry might take the table away from him.

The eye rolled to one side, then fixed again on the ceiling. Dewberry pulled his cap down on his forehead. "Well, I best be getting back home." He sounded tired.

"Let's go to the shed and I'll give you some of the new pears I picked. Haven't had time to wrap them yet."

"No, better be getting back. I'll fetch them later." Dewberry's good eye wasn't even looking at him.

"Now what've you got to do that's so important?"

"Just some things I need to look to. I'll be back in an hour or so for the auction." He zipped his jacket. "We're still going to have a pinochle game tonight, ain't we?"

Orin's skin prickled. "Why wouldn't we?"

"I don't know. Thought maybe you might be busy with something else is all."

"Like what? Come on, say it."

Pointing his pipe stem at Orin, Dewberry started to speak, but instead shuffled through the dining room to the front door. "See you later," he said, tripping the latch.

"And don't you worry," Orin called down the walk after him. "We'll have the game. You tell Misty and Bertha, too, you hear? We're going to have it, just like every Saturday."

He watched until Dewberry reached the street, then turned to get his hat and coat from a chair next to his old table. Sad damn thing, he thought. It was so unsteady you couldn't eat at it for fear of your plate ending up in your lap, and it rocked and wobbled worse than Dewberry trying to get around a corner. A piece of junk, that was all. If he couldn't find nobody to take it, he'd just throw it away, he guessed. He closed his eyes and saw the new table in place. It was so beautiful it made him ache. He hadn't wanted anything so much in a long time, and he felt foolish and awkward, as if he were about to lose his balance, so he thought about all the parties he might have after he bought the table. Why, they could even use it for playing cards, since the one thing he was never going to do was cover it up like the old woman had. He wanted other people to be able to look at it and touch it and admire it with him, to enjoy it as much as he did.

When he went out to take care of his pears, Bertha was on the lawn in front of his table. Her short, fat body crowded the edge as she bent over to inspect it, smearing her finger on the finish, picking at it with her nail.

"You look like an old bulldog sniffing a bone," he said, standing across from her.

"Just wanted to see it close up before I bought it." Her purse dangled like a padlock from her folded arms.

"What?"

"I'm going to buy this table. That old one of mine's all busted and good for nothing." When she smiled, thin lips pulled back from a perfect set of natural teeth, her grey eyes twinkling. "Why? You wasn't thinking of buying it, was you?"

"Hell, no. I wouldn't have this piece of junk on a bet." He spoke quickly to catch her off guard. "Why, look at this. See that chip out of the veneer? And this scraped place." He rocked the table back and forth in a depression in the yard. "And look how damn wobbly it is. You could buy three new tables for the price you'd have to give for this one. I tell you things'll be sky high today. Dew said he seen a bunch of collectors driving around earlier just waiting for the sale to start."

She hadn't budged, that stubborn streak coming up from inside her, hanging in the corner of her eye, dragging it down to the corner of her mouth, her chin, her fallen breasts, on down to her toes that dug into the ground and sprouted roots like a persimmon tree. Her lips pursed, the wrinkled folds greying in the cool air. "You might as well save your breath. You ain't going to talk me out of it. I got my mind made up. If you want it, you'll have to outbid me. That's all."

"I'm trying to tell you, Bertha, I don't want it, but I suppose there'll be a lot of folks who do. I just hope you're willing to pay the price."

"Well, I got the money."

"How much?"

She lowered her purse below the table, her nose twitching. "I'm not about to tell you. You want to know bad enough, you can pay to find out."

"You're like a damn mule running off half-cocked. Why, those fellas from the antique shops'll skin you for every cent. And here's how they'll do it."

"I been to sales before, you don't have to tell me."

"Well, you just listen for a minute." He came around and took her by the arm, walking her away from the table.

"Get your hands off me."

He pulled up short, ready to fend off the purse she was about to swing. "I'm only telling you this for your own good."

"And yours."

"None of mine." She relaxed, the purse hanging from her arm, just inches above the ground. "What I'm trying to explain is that those fellas will wait around until you start the bidding, then come up on you gradual, five, maybe ten dollars at a time to see if you're serious. But they want to keep it low, too. The less they have to spend, the better for them." Her eyes narrowed, the tips of her brows nearly touching. "But—and this is the big thing—they got a lot more money than you do. And they'll use it, too." Her fingers played with the latch on the purse. "Sometimes they get mean about it and drive you way up, and like magic—something they can tell about you without you knowing—they'll stop bidding and leave you with it, a couple hundred dollars poorer. Then they walk away laughing about the sucker."

She aimed her chin at him and folded her arms. "Thank you for the warning, Orin, but that ain't going to happen with me. I set myself an upper limit and I ain't bidding beyond that. Fifty, maybe sixty dollars and that's all. That table ain't worth no more."

"A good idea, Bertha. Just see you stick to your guns about it." He patted her on the shoulder, smiling. "Those fellas can be an ornery bunch. Can't trust them at all. I'd say you set about the right price. Yes, sir, just about right."

Ankles bowing to the breaking point, she waddled off toward the back of the house where the screens on the porch bulged, the back steps tilted to one side, a piece of cross-hatched lattice twisted and leaned toward the ground. Into that picture she walked, getting smaller and smaller. Then at the last moment, as if following an invisible sidewalk, she veered around the corner of the house, out of sight.

Orin went to his table, removed his glove and let his hand rest gently on the satiny surface. It talked to him, a tingle crawling up his fingers, into his elbow, his shoulder, his head, telling him that nobody would ever own it but him.

"You got a pain?" Dewberry said, bad eye squinted shut.

"How long you been standing there?" He slipped his glove on and cleared his throat.

"Just walked up." He put his face close to the table top, as though not to cause Orin any more embarrassment. "So this is what you got your mind set on, is it?"

"Nothing of the kind."

"I seen Bertha. She says she's going to buy it and for me to tell you that you ain't talked her out of nothing." He wiped his hand over the place where his breath had left a wet spot. "Said you was a scoundrel to try and scare her off."

"Now why's that woman so dead set on this table, I'd like to know."

"Guess she figures her old one ain't much good and with this one here she could have folks over once in a while and not be ashamed. Why, she was even talking about us coming over to her house for cards tonight."

"Her house?"

"That's what she said to me just a minute ago." Dewberry pressed down pipe ashes with his finger and wiped it on his pants.

"Damn stubborn old woman, break herself up over this."

"Not from what she told me." He hacked and spit on a tree stump. "Her old man left her pretty well fixed. Several thousand and she don't see it doing no good in the bank. Says she's going to spend it when she decides on something she wants."

"If that don't take gall. Here she's been crying about not even having enough to bring her share of the sweet rolls. That old miser. What's wrong with her anyhow?"

Dewberry knocked his pipe against his heel. "Couldn't say, but she wants that table."

Leading Dewberry by the arm to the shed behind his house, Orin fumbled a key into the lock and wiggled it open. He pushed Dewberry inside and kicked the bottom of the door shut. After pulling down the blinds on the two side windows, he held his ear to the door before clicking the lock.

"Turn the light on," Dewberry said, picking at his eye. "Can't see a damn thing. Don't know why I have to have them pears just now."

"Help me move this."

Dewberry felt his way over to where Orin struggled with a wringer washing machine, grunting it across the uneven floor.

Orin pried up a board. Lifting carefully with both hands, he set the Folgers can between him and Dewberry. He meticulously unrolled each bill, folding it lengthwise so it would lay flat. He made four separate piles, patting them on the ends and sides to keep them straight. What coins there were he left to rattle in the can.

"Nobody's ever seen this before, so you keep your mouth shut."

Dewberry gawked with both eyes.

"There's eighty twenties, thirty-five tens, twenty fives, thirteen ones and some odd cents."

Dewberry shook his head, mouth hanging open. "You wouldn't spend all that."

"If I have to."

"You're crazy, crazy as a goddamn mudhen. You and that old woman. What's so special about that table anyway? With that kind of money you could buy any one you put your mind to."

"But I want that one," Orin said, peering directly into Dewberry's murky eye.

The gavel banged.

Dewberry helped him fold the leaves and carry the table to his house.

After it was in place, Orin sat in his rocker, staring at it. Just staring, to see if it looked as he had imagined it would.

"Well, you got your table." Dewberry chewed the horny flesh on the side of a finger.

"She drove me up, Dew. Goddamn stubborn woman drove me up. Why'd she do that if she was finished? No damn sense in it. Stupid. Pig-headed. Damn snake knows better than to bite itself." Dewberry polished the tabletop with his handkerchief. "After all I done for her, she pulled this. Since her old man died I painted her house, inside and out, mowed her lawn every week, fixed her pipes so they wouldn't freeze up and bust, patched a couple cracks in the basement—and never took a cent from her, not one damn penny. And she drove me up."

"Well, you wanted the table. You got it."

"Damn bitch of a woman. What kind of neighbor is that? Don't give a damn about how I feel. I was going to make her choke on it at a hundred and fifty, make her take it and sit on it, but she done this to me. To hell with her!" He slammed his fist on the arm of the rocker. "Just wait till she wants me to do something again. She'll pay all right."

"What about the game tonight?" Dewberry asked after a long pause, looking up from the end of the table like a child who had been scolded for eating too fast.

Orin rocked, listening to Dewberry's thumbnail pop against his tooth.

"We always have the game, Orin. Been a long time since we ain't. We can't let her keep us from having the game. It just ain't worth that, being mad. He rubbed his hands together nervously, lips twisting at the corners. "Sounds silly maybe, but I ain't sure what I'd do without the game. Just set at home, I guess."

Orin smiled in spite of himself as he got up and pulled Dewberry's cap down until the bill was parallel with his nose. "Don't worry about that, we're going to have it like always. Only this once we'll make it special. A celebration game. We'll celebrate getting the table. Come on, quit moping around and help me plan things."

Dewberry's tongue poked out the corner of his mouth. "Well, the girls said they was bringing sweet rolls."

"We've got to do better than that. This here's going to be a party. Think of some special party goods we can get."

Dewberry licked his lips. "Some cakes. You know, those little frosted ones with cherries and filling."

Orin nodded.

"And some nuts, how about that, Orin, some nuts? I can't eat them very good, but you can."

"Fine."

"And maybe some chips with, um, some dip?" He swallowed.

"Great, great. That's the kind of party I was thinking of."

"And, well, maybe we could get us some wine?" Dewberry pulled at the cuffs of his jacket.

"Hell, yes. How about that, Dew, some wine? We'll, drink us a toast and throw the damn glasses against the wall! It'll be some party. And I'll put some records on the player. You can even dance if you want to." He crumpled the money like dry leaves in his coat pocket.

"And you won't be mad anymore?" Dewberry said.

"Hell, no. It'll be a forgive and forget party, too. Ain't nothing any different now, except I got my table like you said." He ran his finger along its edge. "Well, we better get on down and buy our goods because I got a little special something I been saving we can have before the girls come."

Dewberry wiped his mouth, clouded eye circling with excitement.

When they got back, Orin set the whiskey and glasses on his new table. He poured equal amounts and handed a glass to Dewberry.

"Ain't you going to put a cloth on in case you spill?"

"No. This table's never going to be covered," Orin said, emptying his glass. "Ain't she pretty, though? Prettiest thing I ever seen. That's why I wanted her so bad, because she's pretty. You ever wanted something pretty?"

"Suppose I have." Dewberry held out his glass.

"Then you know what I mean." He nodded to himself and moved the bottle out of Dewberry's reach. "We'd best get things ready."

Once all was arranged, Orin stepped back. "Looks good to me. Why don't you go over and tell the girls about our party. Tell Bertha all's forgiven. I'll set some music on."

Two and a half Red Foley records later Dewberry came back alone.

"Where's the girls?"

Dewberry poured himself a drink. "Said they wasn't coming. And they ain't coming till you apologize. Bertha said she wouldn't never come in this house again till you said you was sorry for driving her up." He bolted the whiskey and made a circle with his finger on the table. "I tried to tell them about the party, how special it was, and that you wasn't mad, but they already had their minds set."

"Why, that sorry old hag. Damn her, she's the one that drove me up! I never heard of such a thing."

"But," he cleared his throat, "didn't you say you was going to dump the table on her? You did say that, Orin."

"That ain't the point. She's the one that needs to apologize."

"Maybe both of you was wrong. Maybe if you just talked it over and said you was sorry we could still have the party. We got to have the party."

Orin glared at the lines of miniature rose arbors spreading across his wallpaper. "No! By God, no!"

"Maybe we could take the party stuff over there."

"No!"

"Please, Orin.".

"You got to understand there's more than that party at stake here."

"What shall I tell them, then?" His good eye was about to weep.

"You know what you can tell them."

Orin picked up his whiskey glass and rocked as Dewberry shut the door.

At eleven he was rocking and drinking alone. The room was dark, except for the glow of the streetlight on the tabletop. The party goods were still in place, dark piles like mud clods.

He put the tips of his fingers on the edge of the table, letting them draw his whole hand on top of it. The surface was smooth and cold. He flinched but made himself keep his hand there. Cold and almost clammy. "Damn silliness," he said, touching the glass to his lips.

Cradling the bottle in the crook of his left arm, he struggled into his coat. He smoothed his gloves down over his fingers one hand at a time and set his hat squarely on his-head.

The moon was up and the few leaves left in trees hung outlined like night birds. The rest scattered around his feet, the breeze flattening them against his rose trellises, the side of his shed, Bertha's trash barrel and the bushes in back of her house.

At her north window he peered through the pane he had replaced. The three of them sat around her old table, a piece of broom handle propping up one leaf. They were playing cards, smiling and talking, the ceiling light pulled down so it shined just on them, and all around it was dark where the night came in. Beside each player was a coffee cup and on the end of the table nearest the window was the lopsided sweet roll basket covered by a red and white checkered cloth. Dewberry's pipe was turned upside down in an ashtray. They all laughed about something, the sound filtering through the glass and dying on the wind. As Dewberry handed the deck to Misty, his crazy eye swung toward Orin.

At the back door he raised his fist to knock, but let it drop. Holding the bottle up against his mouth, he started back across the alley that separated their houses. His looked odd, so closed up and dark. And the one next door, the old woman's, the same.

He found his whiskey glass and a barber shop quartet record in the dark and positioned himself in his rocker, his shoulders thrown back proudly. He drank and hummed to the music, waiting beside his table.

Gary D. Wilson

Falling Out

He sits at the picnic table in the back yard. She stands behind him clicking barber shears. She is thirty-four, bronzed and beach blonde; he is thirty-five with white yet solid flesh and hair the color of mud. No one else has ever cut his hair to suit him, and the role seems to please her.

He jerks his shoulders, arm grazing her bare leg. She bounces back like a ballerina, comb and scissors held high. He resettles into his slouch; she steps up again behind him.

"Why didn't you slap it?" he asks.

Snip. Pause. "What?"

"The mosquito that was biting me."

"I didn't see it." Snip-snip. "Maybe it was hair sticking you."

"I know a bite when I feel one. Now I'll get a welt. I always get a welt."

"We can put baking soda on it," she says. "Or is it vinegar?"

"You should have killed it."

"They say you're supposed to leave them alone, let them drink their fill and buzz off. Then the bite won't itch as much."

"Well, they're wrong. It would itch the same no matter what, since it's the anti-coagulant the mosquito injects that causes the reaction in the first place."

"Mosquito spit?" Snip. Comb. Snip-snip.

"You Arizonans have the oddest notions," he says.

"We had mosquitoes there, too, you know."

"Not real ones. Not like——"

"——in the north woods of Minnesota," she finishes for him, sing-song.

"Except I don't believe we had the roach problem you did. No, I don't remember ever seeing a single one at home."

"I figured it out," she says. "When you smash them like that, it squeezes all their spit into you at once."

A high bright June sun steams the earth, so that even in the shade the air has the faint smell of riverbanks. Kansas City has a climate neither of them likes—so hot in summer there are days when it hurts to take a breath, so cold in winter bones ache and sinuses never clear. But the heartland, as natives call it, is the best compromise they could arrive at, since one of them liked the West Coast and the other the East. Neither cared for the Deep South, the Northwest, Canada or Mexico.

Ten years ago, after finishing graduate school, they accepted teaching positions at Park College (Raymond in languages, Louise in mathematics), bought a Cape Cod house with a glassed back porch and moved in.

On Friday night the first week there they made love in the corner of the yard under an arching elm. The next morning they bought tulip bulbs and planted them in the shape of sleeping lovers. Over time the design lost its original curves, growing more and more rectangular. That same day, in the afternoon, she began cutting his hair, a weekly ritual they have kept with unfailing devotion.

"You're still angry about last night, aren't you, Raymond?"

"Not at all. It's settled as far as I'm concerned. You now have your Bach, I have my Beethoven. You have your Benedictine, I have my White Horse. You have your Russell, I have my Proust. Why, you even have your anchovies, and I have my pepperoni.

You have your Lifeboy, I have my Dial, you have your new job, I have my—"

"There, you see? You are, aren't you?"

"I-don't-get-angry, Louise."

"Maybe if you did," she says. "Maybe if you let it out all at once—"

"A la mashed mosquito?"

Snip-snip, as if he has not spoken. Snip. A perfect arc of flesh being laid bare behind his ear.

"Is letting it all out, as you say, another aspect of this Mock Transverse Theory of Coping you've become so enamored with?"

"Block," she says. "Not Mock. And you really should give him more of a chance. He's a very nice man."

"You make him sound like your father—except that on occasion you also tell me what sad eyes he has."

"He does, but I don't see—"

"Well, it's hardly a term one would use to describe a parent."

"You're jealous."

"Jealousy is a waste of energy, Louise."

"So is washing clothes, cooking, shopping, cleaning."

"Loving?" he asks.

"Don't pervert what I say because you're out of sorts."

"Am I? Am I, really?"

"You got up feeling mean and nasty and haven't improved a bit."

"It's fascinating," he says, "how two people's perceptions can differ so much."

"And if we can't be decent," thrusting the comb past his ear like a pointer, "maybe we shouldn't be around each other at all."

"I suppose I could take a vow of silence for the rest of the day," he says.

"Please don't. You make a terrible martyr."

"My God, I had no idea I was such an irritant." Snip-snip. Comb. Fluff. Snip.

"I don't really think you've been yourself for some time now. Do you?" She runs her hand over the side of his head, as if molding clay.

"Can't honestly say, since I find the subject of my mental health totally boring."

"Well, it seems to me that you've been more depressed and more irascible than usual. And I can't remember when I last saw you smile."

"A month ago, wasn't it?"

The scissors stop. "I didn't specify a time, did I?"

"I thought so."

"Strange. Why a month, Raymond?"

"I don't know. Make it two weeks. Two months. A year. Whatever you want."

"It was a month yesterday that I announced my resignation."

"Is that right? I hadn't realized."

"I thought we had talked all that through."

"We have, we have."

"But you don't seem satisfied yet," she says.

"Nonsense. You had no choice. A promotion, a healthy raise, moving from a college to a university. Just because I would have had trouble doing what Block did doesn't mean he should have. He's your chairman now. He can do whatever he can get by with, and if that happens to include raiding the department here on his way out, so be it. That's the name of the game. Administrative politics at its finest. Can't blame a person for that. No, I'm just a diehard romantic when it comes to Park. As long as they want me I'll probably stay."

"Am I to feel complimented or accused?" she says.

"That is a problem."

"But it shouldn't be, not if you really do feel all right about my leaving."

"I do, Louise, I do. Now does that settle the matter?"

"Because it isn't like I'm marrying Jerry Block or anything."

"Oh, that business again. No, I've always considered him a rather rumpled old turnip. Ouch!"

"Sorry. The scissors caught."

"Do you mind scratching? In the middle. There. Harder. Harder. Thank you. Is there a welt?"

"A small one."

"I told you. Miserable creatures. Maybe we should move the barbershop to the back porch."

"But we've always come out here."

"Nothing is written in stone," he says.

"It's just so much trouble. We'd have to move the porch furniture and set up your chair every time, and then I'd still bump into things as I worked around. Not to mention how spotty the light is from the louvers."

"I suppose you're right."

"There's just no sense changing everything for the sake of one little bite."

"I said I suppose you're right." Comb. Comb. Snip. Comb. Snip-snip.

"But we are going to do something with that flower garden," he says.

"It's the trees and the hedge. There's even grass back there now. What we need to do is give it a good weeding, maybe cull a few bulbs. Redefine it."

"Ah, the mathematical mind."

"Head down." She takes the brush from the white cloth spread on the table and whips up a thick lather in the mug. "Farther. Stretch."

The lather is cool and rich on the back of his neck, her finger marking a line down from his ear, the straight razor deftly following pass after pass. Never once has she nicked him, never once has she made light of his vulnerability. But in the middle of the next to last stroke, she pauses, and at that instant he sees in his mind's eye the precise angle of the blade, the neat indentation it makes in his skin. Despite himself, he shivers.

She wrings out a washcloth, wipes his neck and dries it. "There we are. All done."

He carries the sheet that was over him toward the tree, shakes the shorn hair glistening into the breeze, and goes inside to have a look in the bathroom mirror.

"It's too short," he says, reemerging.

"No, it isn't. Turn around."

"It's too goddamn short!"

"I really don't know what you're talking about, Raymond. It looks the same as ever to me."

For Those Who Favor Fire

A rubber tip was gone from one leg of the stepstool. It screeched as she pulled it to the workbench—a witch's shriek, a cat's yowl—a thin white line on the concrete, the mark she'd been worried about leaving there finally for everyone to see. She reached down, a finger extended as if to touch a fresh wound. It was cold and hard, a bloodless cut. She took it as a sign.

The antifreeze was on the shelf above the workbench. NAPA brand, the only kind he'd have. One thing about Cecil, he never cut corners when it came to his car. He was a mechanic and always said a sure way to ruin a motor was to be cheap about it. And in this case she had to admit she was glad he was so fussy. It was nicer to be able to think about giving him something he liked.

She'd figured out what to do from reading a book at the library. Ethylene glycol, it said, is a clear, syrupy, colorless liquid, slightly sweet to the taste, which is most commonly used in the production of antifreeze. She remembered putting the book down and smiling, then worrying that someone might see her and guess what she was thinking. Ingesting as little as three or four ounces, the book went on—a mere half cup—would be plenty to kill a man Cecil's size. What could be simpler than that?

There was a sign in bright red letters on the back of the plastic bottle:

WARNING
HARMFUL OR FATAL IF SWALLOWED

Do not drink antifreeze or solution.
If swallowed, induce vomiting immediately.
Call a physician.

KEEP OUT OF REACH OF CHILDREN
AND ANIMALS

And husbands? she wondered. Wives? Jilted lovers? But life was full of warnings, both given and taken. Hadn't he said himself that things were going to hell in a handbasket? And he wasn't talking about the world. He was talking about them. He was warning her, just as the sign was warning her. It might be harmful or fatal if things continued the way they were. She'd tried to imagine what it would be like, going to hell in a handbasket. Little piles of them, each topped by a China doll head in their own likeness with bright unblinking eyes, in a basket of delicate weave. But who would be carrying it? And would the person know that in their case hell had to be cold? Heat might revive them. Heat wasn't what they were suffering from.

She lifted down the bottle and set it on the workbench. It seemed heavier than the day Cecil showed her how to remove the child-resistant cap, how to pour it into the car with a funnel to keep from getting it all over the engine and herself, how to know when to stop. He'd told her he wanted her to have an idea where things were and what to do with them in case anything ever happened to him. And he was good at explaining how things worked. Machines he could tear down and look at, with parts he could replace if they were worn out or broken.

He wasn't nearly so good with people. "What's wrong with you?" he would ask, but it never seemed to matter how she answered, if at all. He would stare hard at her, eyes narrowing in concentration, as if trying to see inside her, find out where the defective valve was, the bad bearing he could fix and, giving her a good turn, set everything right again. He never once seemed to consider that the problem could be inside him, that maybe he had a malfunctioning thermostat that had cooled him off to the point he was in danger of freezing up, and it was her duty now to help save him.

She carefully unscrewed the cap on the antifreeze and poured out exactly half a jar. It was a small mixing jar with ounces marked on one side and milliliters on the other. The book had mentioned how many milliliters per kilogram it would take, but those measurements didn't mean anything to her. They only confused her, threw her off, tilted her to one side where she knew if she stayed too long and thought too much, she'd end up dizzy. She might fall then and drop the jar. Wouldn't that be a mess? And one fear she constantly harbored was of going to the garage—Cecil's own special place—and doing something terribly wrong. Breaking something that couldn't be fixed or making a mess that couldn't be cleaned up. A mark was one thing, a mess was another. So she put milliliters and kilograms out of her mind completely. She knew ounces. She'd grown up with them. She could trust them.

She'd always trusted Cecil too. Not to do anything silly. Anything that would hurt himself, her, them. To her knowledge, he never had. Nothing she knew of, could prove. And that was the most maddening. The waiting to see when he would. Everyone did sooner or later, didn't they? Wasn't that the way things were? Wasn't that how life was lived now, just sitting around waiting for the end to come, knowing with absolute certainty that it would? Because people went through changes, she'd read. They warmed up and cooled off at different times, and while it was rare enough that two people arrived at a neutral point simultaneously, it was nearly impossible to maintain such equilibrium once it was reached.

But they had. Until just recently. At least that was how she saw it. Right from the beginning, when he first touched her beneath a lilac bush in her parents' yard, the grass dark and lush, damp-smelling, his arm hooking around her, drawing her close, pulling her to him as his hand traveled her side one rib at a time, a train over bad track, up the hill and home.

They'd known love. They'd made sparks aplenty. Smoke and fire too, for that matter. She had never been able to imagine anyone she would rather hold, anyone she would rather have look at her in that way that made her insides melt. She knew love all right. Love is patient, love is kind. Love believes all things, hopes all things, endures all things. And no greater love has any woman than that she save a man from himself. Save him from going cold like a slab of rock releasing its heat into night after endless night.

Of course the same thing was happening all around her. In the movies, on television, in the papers. Next door. There wasn't a single couple amongst all their friends and neighbors who were still married. But what did that say about people? Didn't they care what happened? Was it just too much effort to carry on together? Or to do what needed to be done before the situation reached that point?

She stepped back up on the stool, slid the antifreeze into place and stepped down. Even though there was no need to, she wiped the workbench, then set the stool back where it belonged. Satisfied, except for the line on the floor, which she still found curiously reassuring, she turned toward the utility room door.

How odd, she thought, pausing at the garage window. How green. She supposed they needed to make it some color, but why green, she wondered, holding the jar up. And why this green of tree leaves in sunlight? The color was so intense it seemed as though someone had distilled the essence of all light and all leaves and put it in the bottle. All life. Put it in the bottle and shook it up and said some words over it or worked some equations and made it so strong that even a couple of sips was too much.

She lowered the jar. She had a lot to get done—a meal to cook, a bed to make, a bath to take. She didn't have time to be standing around like that. If she wasn't careful, he'd be home before she knew it, sniffing around for his food, getting cranky when it wasn't there. And she didn't want that to happen. Not tonight.

In the kitchen, she opened the refrigerator, cleared a space at the back of the second shelf and set the jar in just so, not touching the walls or any of the leftovers. It seemed silly even to her to keep antifreeze in a refrigerator, but she'd thought it through and decided that that probably was the best place. Cecil didn't cook. He didn't snack between meals. He might drink a beer or two of an evening, but they were always in the door rack, so he never had reason to look in. To her mind it was the perfect place, and she couldn't help smiling as she closed the door at how well everything was going.

Pan fried catfish, parslied new potatoes, fresh green beans, rhubarb pie. She untaped the menu from the refrigerator and threw it away. The pie was ready. The fish were thawed. They were ones he'd caught himself on an overnight trip to the river not long ago. Perfect size, rolled in corn meal, just the way he liked them best. And tea. She couldn't forget tea. With lemon and sugar. He could drink a gallon on a hot day.

She prepared the potatoes and put them in the oven. She washed a few dishes and wiped down the counter. She put water on to boil. At a quarter to five she went to make the bed.

The sheets were from her grandmother. She'd never used them because they were so fine, with hand-embroidered flower borders and matching pillow cases. But now there was no reason not to. If she didn't put them on now, she never would. She tucked the corners nice and tight, fluffed the pillows an extra time or two, double-checked the spread to make sure it was straight.

"Yes," she heard herself say, standing in the doorway, cocking her head this way and that. Just what she'd imagined, and she turned back down the hall.

She took the water off the stove and dropped tea bags in to steep. Tea leaves, tree leaves. She slid the oven rack out and forked the potatoes. She got the pan of green beans from the refrigerator and put it on the burner where the water had been. She heated oil in the skillet and laid the fish in. When one side had browned, she turned them over. The tea was ready. She poured it into a pitcher of ice cubes and set it in the refrigerator. She removed the fish from the skillet, draining them on paper towels. Then she put them in a covered baking dish, reset the oven to WARM and scooted the fish in next to the potatoes. She lifted the lid on the pan of green beans, stirred them, adjusted the flame and left for her bath.

She liked the way her legs looked after she shaved them. She liked how bath oil beads made her skin slick but not greasy, smelling of lilac petals drying in the sun. She lay back in the water, her head on the rim of the tub. Warmth enveloped her like a body; and for a moment she could feel him, his weight, his breath on her neck.

She woke with a start. Her reflection in the door mirror stared back, but with no recognition, as if the image didn't really belong to her, as if it had stumbled into the room accidentally, into the wrong life.

She glanced away. The clock on the dresser said a quarter to six. She got out quickly, dried off and dressed.

Returning to the kitchen, she drained the green beans, buttered them and put them in the oven. Everything was ready, and at precisely six o'clock she heard Cecil's truck pull into the driveway.

He had always been punctual. It was a matter of pride with him to be places on time, not to keep people waiting, not to have to rush because he hadn't planned ahead. Dependable. That was the word. Cecil was dependable. You could count on him, like a good clock or a well-tuned motor.

The garage door opened. He never used the front entrance. It was for strangers and visitors who didn't know better. She could almost see him, lean and hard in his blue uniform, sleeves rolled above two dark moles on his right forearm that looked for all the world like grease spots he'd forgotten to wash off. He would be standing there now, the way he always did, staring back down the drive and out into the neighborhood. After a while, depending on what he'd seen or been thinking about, he would close the door and come on in, a trip that rarely took more than a few seconds.

But now a full minute had passed. Maybe two. Why was he taking so long? What could he possibly be doing?

"Here." He looked sheepish, childishly awkward in his stocking feet, holding a bouquet of roses out to her.

"You remembered," she said.

"Figured I'd be in trouble if I didn't," he smiled.

"Let me get a vase."

There was something different about him. She couldn't put her finger on what exactly, but he seemed more relaxed, more playful, giving her flowers even, as though he was also about to be relieved of some great burden. And it suddenly struck her— shoulders and head dipping from the blow—that he could just as easily be planning to get rid of her.

"Cecil!" she half-shouted, whirling to face him.

He peered at her, brow and mouth twisted into a question mark.

"Would you mind setting these on the table for me?" she said, handing him the vase.

The possibility had never crossed her mind. It simply never had. That wasn't his style. To announce that things had gone to hell, let some time pass, then drop the bomb, tell her he was leaving, that he wanted a divorce—that was how he would go about it. And he would start just like this. Bringing her flowers on their anniversary, softening her with smiles and his little boy ways. Had he kissed her yet? Touched her? That would be next. Anything to put her off guard and leave her vulnerable. And when he saw she was, then he'd do it. Then he would hit and run for all he was worth. The bastard.

"Umm. What did I do to deserve this?" he said, gazing into the oven.

Damn him. Damn him to hell.

"A special day calls for a special meal, don't you think?" She willed her voice to an even pitch, brought a smile to her mouth. She had to stay in control. She couldn't let her anger ruin things now. "Everything's ready, so why don't you go get cleaned up."

"Okay." He turned to leave. That is, his body turned, not his feet, and he swiveled back toward her, mouth open to speak.

"Go on," she told him before he could say anything. She didn't want to hear it. No matter what it was. She just didn't want to hear it.

He nodded and looked down, socks matted against his arches, bright white below the shoe line, then nodded again and leaned a shoulder into the hallway, as if pushing open an invisible door.

She listened for the first rush of water from the shower before going to set the table.

She used their best china and silverware, polishing each piece as she put it in place. She lit candles, straightened the napkins, scooped up a fern leaf from beside the vase.

Pipes in the basement clanked when he shut off the water. The shower door slid open. He coughed. He would be standing naked now beside the tub, dark hair like a shadow over his body.

She put the fish and potatoes on the table and went back for the green beans.

A bureau drawer whumped shut.

She adjusted the serving dishes, moved the candles a bit to the right and stepped back to study the arrangement.

Dressed in a clean white undershirt and underpants, he would be combing his hair in front of the door mirror, checking the part, maybe fingering a cut on his jaw from shaving. She doubted that he would find anything unusual about his reflection.

She poured two glasses of tea, leaving room in his for antifreeze.

The closet door banged.

Her hand trembled as she took the jar from the refrigerator. But not from fear, she realized. She was excited. She was like a schoolgirl waiting to go on a date with someone she'd not been out with before and wondering how it would be. Was she wearing the right thing? Would he like her? Would he try to hold her hand or kiss her?

He would be dressed now in the red plaid shirt she liked and his tan pants, and he would be sitting on the edge of the bed tying his shoes. When he got up, he wouldn't straighten the spread.

She poured a third of the antifreeze into his glass—she was certain he would have at least two refills in the course of the meal—and added a few extra drops of lemon juice to cover any off-taste. She then floated a mint leaf in her own glass to ensure she could tell which was which. He hated mint and she liked it, so it would seem perfectly normal.

He joined her just as she was setting the tea on the table.

He was even more handsome out of uniform, hair a sharp dark line around his ear and along his neck. Had he been to the barber recently? She couldn't remember to save herself. And he had shaved, his face clear and smooth as her legs. No cuts. And the cologne he'd used was what she'd bought for his birthday. She was glad he liked it.

"Well," he said, pulling out her chair. How long had it been since he'd done that? He usually sat down at the same time she did and ate without looking up, their conversations consisting mainly of questions with one-word answers. Yet here he was now, on top of everything else, tea glass raised in a toast: "To ten more."

She drank, choking.

"It's not that horrible to think about, is it?"

She passed him the fish.

His tea glass was still full. Had her coughing interrupted him? Was there something about the appearance of it, or the smell?

"Isn't that what you're supposed to say? If you've had ten, wish for ten more?"

"I don't know that much about toasts," she said.

"Yeah, well—"

"How was work today?"

"Same as usual."

"Is that good or bad?"

"Neither." His plate was filled. He still hadn't touched the tea. "It's a job. You go do it and come home, get up and go do it again."

"A lot of people would probably be happy for that much."

"Yeah, a lot of people."

She could feel him looking at her, his eyes resting like a hand on the side of her face.

"Makes you think, is all, after a while." He talked around the food he had pushed into his cheek like a plug of tobacco. "Makes you wonder if this is how things are going to be in another ten years."

She knew she was supposed to say something. Some comforting words about how it was all going to work out, he'd see, if he just kept in there, kept his spirit and didn't give up. But how could she? How could she offer encouragement about a future that was never going to be?

"I don't know, Cecil. There really isn't much you can do about it one way or the other, is there?"

He leaned forward, elbows spread on the table, a look of pleasant surprise on his face, as if she'd given him the very opening he'd been searching for.

"Why, there's lots of things. You could quit your job, for starters. Find a new one. Move to a new place. Meet new people. Or if that didn't work out, you could—"

She waited for him to finish, just as she waited for his outstretched hand to close on the tea glass. But he neither spoke nor drank. He was like a cat playing with a mouse, teasing it nearly to death before getting to the point. Was he smiling? She couldn't bear to look at him.

"What's wrong?" he said.

"Nothing."

"You sure?"

"Yes."

"I didn't mean to upset you."

"You didn't." She hoped her own smile was convincing. He shrugged and picked up the glass.

She shut her eyes.

He coughed with his mouth closed. His face reddened. Tears ran down his cheeks. He swallowed what he could and coughed again.

"What the hell!" he blurted when his voice was back.

"Take another drink. That'll help." Did she sound normal? She could hardly hear herself or him for the ringing in her ears.

He sipped cautiously, took a larger drink, then held the glass away, examining it.

"It's a new tea," she said. "I hope you like it."

"Not bad once you get by the first drink." He seemed to be waiting for her to laugh. She didn't. "A little too lemony, maybe."

"That's my fault."

"No, it's all right. Really." And he downed the rest of the glass as if to prove his sincerity. "Except I still think I like Lipton's better."

With that, he fell to eating like a man whose conscience was suddenly clear. He cleaned his plate and refilled it, cleaned it again and took a third helping of potatoes, but only finished part of them. Then settling back and sucking at his teeth a moment, he held out his empty glass and asked if she would get him more.

She felt strangely honored by his request, as though he had become her unwitting ally in doing what needed to be done, and she solemnly prepared the second serving with only half as much lemon.

"Great meal," he said as she set the glass in front of him. His face was more relaxed, his gaze less fixed.

"I'm glad you liked it," she said. And she was. A nice dinner was the least she could do.

He toyed with the glass a long while, picking it up, sipping the tea, nibbling really, as if savoring the flavor, then putting the glass down and turning it slowly on the table, wiping the sweat from its sides a stroke at a time with his finger, the same as she'd seen him do with cocktail glasses and beer mugs.

"There's rhubarb pie for dessert," she said.

He looked up and grinned. Crookedly, she thought. Even lewdly. The book said initial symptoms of poisoning mimic those of alcoholic intoxication. But she had no idea. Even though she was seeing it happen—Cecil getting drunker by the minute—she still couldn't help being surprised, as if she had never truly believed it would work.

"Would you like it now or later?" she asked.

"What?" There was no doubt about the meaning of that grin.

"The pie, Cecil."

"I was thinking. . . ." He looked puzzled, blinking at her, as though she might know what he'd been about to say. "I was thinking of something a little different for dessert."

"I'm sure you were, and all in good time. But I didn't go to the trouble of baking this pie just to have it go to waste."

"It'll keep."

"So will you."

He raised his head, tipping it back imperiously as she'd seen him do only once or twice before when she wouldn't let him drive afterwards, an awful sneer on his lips that made her want to slap him. "Stuff it then!" he said, although maybe not as forcefully as he might have liked, since his mouth seemed suddenly full of his tongue. "Just stuff it!" And with a final indignant flourish, he swept up his drink, gulped the rest down and slammed the glass on the table.

He sat glowering at his knees while she cleared the dishes, cut the pie and poured more tea, mixing his with the remainder of the antifreeze but no lemon.

When she returned to the dining room, she found him slumped forward in his chair.

"Cecil?" she called, afraid he might be asleep. He peered up at her, eyes glassy red.

"Are you all right?"

"Whadda you care?"

"I hope you like the pie."

He forked a piece but didn't eat it.

"It has just the right tartness for me," she said.

He squinted until he found her. "Some fun party. That's all I can say."

She looked away. "I'm sorry you don't like it."

"Some fun pie."

"Now that's not fair, Cecil. You haven't even tasted it yet."

He put the bite in his mouth, washing it down with tea. "Wasn't no good to begin with. Can't be no goddamn good now."

She stood, shaking her head. She had no intention of getting involved in this kind of endless argument. Not at this point. She began clearing the table.

He stared at her, a mixture of anger and confusion in his eyes—maybe even the first hint of fear, she couldn't be sure—but he seemed unable to do anything about it, his head dropping back down, wobbling uselessly at the end of his neck as he mumbled on and on like some poor misunderstood drunk unable to find anyone to listen to his troubles.

She carried the dishes to the kitchen and stayed, watching him from the doorway. She wasn't certain how long she was there. But it didn't really matter because it was where she needed to be. She had distance now. She had time. All she had to do was be patient and he would come to see for himself soon enough how wrong he'd been.

He tried to stand. Slowly, deliberately, as though testing his balance with each movement. He caught himself as he fell, but not in time, the chair nearly going over backwards with him. His head hung pathetically to one side, mouth drawn down, face pale.

"Aileen?" A child crying out in the night.

"Aileen!"

"There's no need to yell. I'm right here."

"Sick."

She got him up, draping his arm over her shoulder, and walked him to the hall bathroom.

"I'm sorry," she said. She hated for anyone to be so miserable. Especially to vomit like that.

She waited outside the door, counting off the list of symptoms in her mind like ingredients in a recipe: intoxication, nausea, vomiting, stupor, convulsions, death. Could death really be called a symptom? It seemed to her more like a condition.

When he had finished, she went in. His mouth gaped. His eyes were wide and wildly fearful.

"Let me get you a washcloth."

He crawled away, collapsing before he reached the door.

"Let me help you."

He was so limp she had to drag him to the bedroom. She dropped him on the floor.

"What's wrong with you, Cecil?"

He pulled himself to his knees at the foot of the bed.

"That's better. Come on, now, get undressed." He was crying.

"For pity's sake, Cecil, let me."

She undressed him and pulled the covers down.

He sat on the edge of the bed, as if uncertain what to do next.

She lifted his feet. He kicked at her.

"Bitch!" he sobbed, clutching the mattress with both hands, like someone trying to wake up from a nightmare. Did he see the scratch on the floor? The white NAPA bottle on the dark shelf? Could he read the warning label?

He sighed and fell over. She raised his feet and covered him.

In the kitchen, she put the food away and washed the dishes, including the empty antifreeze jar, which she then buried at the bottom of the trash bag. There was no hurry now. She wiped off the counter and stove. She hosed out the sink. She folded the tea towel and hung it on the rack. She squeezed out the dishcloth one last time and laid it over the faucet.

She locked the doors, turned off the lights and checked to be sure the coffee pot was unplugged.

She went to the bedroom, undressed and brushed her teeth.

He seemed so peaceful.

She got into bed carefully to keep from rousing him.

His head rolled toward her, eyes closed.

"Aileen?" she thought he asked in a muffled, dreamy voice.

Her heart swelled. She felt like crying herself. "I'm here." She moved next to him, sliding her leg over his, pulling his hand to her breast. "It's me."

And it always had been her. She knew that now. And it always would be. She'd been in time. Just in the nick of time.

He seemed to be sobbing.

"There, there."

"Ai—!"

He was erect, his whole body rigid, shaking, hand tearing at her breast as he lurched beside her.

It would be the first of many, she knew, so she eased herself on top of him.

"There now."

To help keep him warm.

"It's only me."

Small Talk

Every afternoon when the sun laid the door's shadow into bright squares on the grey floorboards, ruling a line just short of the back of the last booth, Estelle could glance over her shoulder, regardless of what she was doing, whether behind the bar or in the storeroom, and find him quietly waiting, elbows spread on the worn, rounded collar of the counter. Like clockwork, she would think. Like he had a clock in him that said when it was time. She amused herself off and on by imagining his insides as wheels and springs and gently moving parts, a soft buzzer connected to his brain. She could see him rising from his chair at the sound, putting on his old brown coat and felt hat and walking slowly to the bar.

He wouldn't come in if anyone else was at the counter. She had seen him outside the door, hands on either side of his face to shade the glare, dark eyes roaming the room. If it was clear, except maybe for an old man or a moon-eyed couple at a back table, he would ease onto the second stool from the end of the bar and she would settle a hip on another stool across from him and they would talk. He would stay, beer foam drying on his thin lip, until the after-work crowd arrived. Then, without a word, he would slide a fifty-cent tip toward her and leave.

Out of habit she turned. His seat was empty. Little soft-footed creatures ran up the walls of her stomach, and she sucked in a deep breath, holding it until the feeling went away.

His name was John Jacobs. Once another customer had called him J. J. in passing, but he didn't like it. She could tell by his smile, a quick flick of the lips, like a wink. If she hadn't been for some reason looking at his mouth she would have missed it. He hadn't used it to mock the person or make him feel bad, but more to fill in the silence that came before he said kindly, almost thoughtfully, as if he were about to sweep the checkerboard with a single move, "It's John."

She'd read in a magazine about how a person was supposed to look like his name, and she remembered at the time thinking what a bunch of silliness. Foolishness. She didn't look like Estelle. She could never be that graceful and proper. As far as she could make out nobody looked like their name.

Except maybe for John. It wasn't exactly that he looked like John more than any other John, but whenever she heard the name he came to her mind.

He was a plain man with brown hair and brown eyes and a face so ordinary she wouldn't have paid a bit of attention to him if she'd seen him on the street. But after he'd been coming in for awhile she started noticing certain things about him. Take his nose. It grew straight from between his eyes, almost to a point, nostrils curving back toward his cheeks and into troughs that arched down to the corners of his mouth. Around his right eye crow's feet were heavy as scars. When he smiled, it was the right side of his face. The same when he frowned. When he was thinking about something, he might squint that eye shut and pucker his lips until he figured out what it was he wanted to say. Once the idea was ready, he would scoop it up between his narrow palms and offer it to her, maybe nudging it a little with a slender finger. He was finished when his palms rested on the counter, the veins on the backs of his hands running like rivers deep in a forest.

Delicate, she thought. That was the only word she could come up with. She smiled. Delicate. But nicely so, gentle and kind and thoughtful. Men weren't like that very often.

She'd overheard people saying she was in love with him, that they were having an affair. Stupid talk. She wasn't in love with him at all. She could honestly say she had never really wanted to go to bed with him, and that was what everybody meant when they said love. There wasn't any of that kind of thing with him, either. He'd never once made a pass at her, like some of the other men had. They just talked, usually not about anything very serious at that. He never went on and on for hours about things she didn't care to understand. He didn't get loud and argue. He didn't sit and cry. He didn't act tough and roughhouse around until he got sick or broke something. He would simply slide onto the stool and order a beer while he glanced quickly at the door and longer into the darkened back of the bar. Then he might ask after her and her family, comment on the weather—that it was either too hot or too cold and that spring and fall always seemed somehow to lose out—and after that start on a joke or a story in a soft voice as clear to her as ice snapping.

She sighed, watching a corner of sunlight inch up a table leg beyond the last booth. She missed him; she admitted it. If that was love, she thought, then all right it was, but it didn't hurt a thing.

Through the years she felt she had gotten to know him better than anyone she'd ever met—better than her husband or her kids or her sister Ester or her brother Frank. And that was really all it was—a feeling—because when she looked back on it there wasn't anything about him she could say for a sure fact.

One time, not too long after he'd started coming, she said out of curiosity, wondering how he managed to be there the same time every day, "You work the second shift at the trailer plant?"

Eyebrows pinched, he stared at her.

"What do you do?" she asked, raising her voice the way she would if he were a foreigner.

"What do you mean do?" he said.

"Where do you work?"

He smiled.

"How do you make a living?" she asked.

"I do what I do," he said matter of factly, and that was it.

From then on she put together what she could of his life from bits he let drop during their talks. It was like trying to piece a quilt someone else had cut without knowing what pattern they had in mind. She was never certain she had it worked out right.

She guessed he came from somewhere in the southwest, say New Mexico. Once he mentioned Santa Fe and hesitated, right eye squinted shut, as though there was something he wanted to remember or would rather forget. As far as she could tell, he left home when he was young, maybe even before he finished school, although she had trouble believing that. He knew so much and talked so well he had to have spent a long time in school, or read a lot, or been born smart. No matter what she asked him about, he had an answer. But she had to be careful because he might start on a bunch of malarky, just to pull her leg, which happened with his story about lungfish.

"Sure, lungfish," he said. "Mudfish? Dipnoans? That's their biological name. It comes from the Greek—two breathed—and for a good reason. They have gills and lungs. They need them, too, because when their pools dry up they have to travel overland to find new water. They use their front fins like feet." He walked his hands across the counter. "They're all over around here. Every year during the hottest part of the summer they come

92

from the outlying areas to the river. Like lemmings. You know about lemmings. Sometimes you can hear them at night sliding down the bank and smacking the water. When you're real close, and if you don't frighten them, you can honest to god hear them take a last big gasp of air before they dive in. It's quite a treat, but you have to be patient. Get a good out of the way spot and stay put. I say that because you're going to get restless—it's happened to me—and you'll think they're not coming. But that's always when they do, right when you're about to give up."

"Well I'll be," she said.

"You don't believe me."

"I could swear that was almost word for word what a friend of mine told me once about how to catch snipes."

"Suit yourself, " he said, poker face dissolving into a display of white teeth as fine and straight as his nose and hands.

She was never able to put her finger on exactly how old he was. Maybe forty or fifty or sixty. He was the kind who could have been ten years older or younger than he looked, depending on how he'd lived. One thing for sure, he'd seen a lot in his time. He talked about Dallas, New Orleans, Kansas City, San Francisco, Mexico City, Chicago, London, Paris, Rome, Cairo and other cities she'd never heard of. He described restaurants and streets, the weather and the people, famous buildings and monuments and other things so well she believed he'd been everywhere he said. He couldn't have learned all that from books.

Never once, though, in the whole time she knew him, did she hear a word about his family or friends or what it was that brought him to a small Iowa river town. "It looked like a nice place to rest," was the most he ever said.

She couldn't imagine how he could rest where he was living. He had mentioned in passing a couple of times how noisy the trains were at night, which would put him on the west side of town where ROOMS signs were lined up like hitchhikers along the street. It was a depressing neighborhood with old men and a few old women rocking away the days on latticed porches or wandering in the park a couple of blocks farther west. Even worse, she thought, would be having to stay inside during bad weather, alone in a tiny room with a bed and chair and small table, bathroom down the hall. A person like him needed space. She knew if you kept a good houseplant in the same pot too long, it stopped doing anything but collecting dust on its leaves.

Sunlight so bright it was almost painful poured over the tabletop, drying the damp shadows around Spivey and McCullough in their corner booth. They raised twisted faces toward the light, and she turned away, eyes pausing at the empty stool. All right, she told herself, stop moping around like some high school girl and get to work. Even if he wasn't coming, the others would be in in a few minutes, thirsty and full of vinegar. She did have a business to run.

As always, though, while she was scrubbing and rinsing a tray of dirty glasses and before she realized what had happened, she was thinking about him again.

At first she figured he was a down and outer who just drifted from place to place. She'd seen them before, the hard luck people. She imagined he had been a professor of some kind or a businessman with a wife and kids tucked away in a fancy house like the ones at the edge of town. Then something happened. He commenced to drinking and carousing around, or she did, and the bottom fell out. Here he came, on his ear, and started talking to her, Estelle, because it gave him something to look forward to.

The more she thought about it, though, that idea didn't make sense. He wasn't the depressed type. In fact, he was usually right on top of things. And he never seemed to be out of money, which most times was the case with drifters.

From there, she got the notion he was some kind of odd-ball millionaire who went around the country living in this town and that, trying to find somebody to talk to. He was probably an only child with rich parents who farmed him out to a school or someplace when he was young. Now that his parents were dead, money was all he had, and he'd found her, Estelle, in a small-town bar where, to his mind, with a fifty-cent piece he could buy her attention for an hour or two. The money didn't make her mad because it was his way of saying thanks for the company.

Then, again, maybe he was one of those artists. Several years ago a painter, who was a lot like John Jacobs, had lived in the town. He kept mostly to himself and told people he worked, even though nobody ever saw what came of it. Somehow, though, he had enough money to keep going. That one, the artist idea, appealed to her the most of any.

Lifting a glass, she smiled at how funny all that would sound if she said it to somebody, which she would never do. She only thought about such nonsense to help pass the time. Usually she did like to know as much as she could about people—who they were or what they were or where they came from—because then the people were more real to her. And that way she didn't have to spend her energy filling in the gaps herself, not sure for a minute whether any of it was so. But it was different with him. There were times before when, out of pure frustration, she had wanted to crawl inside him, maybe for only a few seconds, so she could see things through his eyes, think his thoughts, feel what he was all about. She knew she couldn't do that, though. And she wasn't sure she would, even if she was able to. It was his business what he told her and what he didn't. She had finally decided that all she needed was what she saw and heard and thought about him, because the important part was just having him there, talking quietly about whatever came to mind.

As she upended a glass and screwed it down on the brush, she felt the room darken. Against her better judgement, against all her instincts, she glanced at the door, expecting not a passing cloud but him blocking the window with his baggy brown coat, his hands to either side of his face. Light repooled on the table, slanting from it onto the worn floor by the back wall. The soft-footed creatures spun her stomach like a wire cage, and no amount of deep breathing would tame them.

Sure, she'd heard the stories about the man they found in the river. Who hadn't? It was all anybody talked about for a week. A couple of fishermen going out early one morning to check their trotlines down by Turner's bend spotted something caught in the branches of a fallen elm tree. At first, as they told it, they didn't pay any attention. The sun wasn't up yet and the fog was pretty thick. They went on pulling in their lines, thinking it was an old log or plastic bag hung up there. Then they both heard a bubble break the surface and were looking right at it when the body rolled over. Like to scared the bejesus out of them. There they were not ten yards from a dead man—and the only way they could even be sure of that was by how he was dressed. The fish and turtles had been to him already. They always stopped at that point and looked away, shaking their heads. "Not a pretty sight," was all the more they would say.

People started asking her right away if she'd seen that "John fella" lately. "No," she would say. "But then I don't keep him on a leash either."

As talk grew, the more sure everybody was that the man they'd found was John Jacobs. It all fit, they said. He hadn't been seen since the day the body was discovered and as far as they could tell he matched the description of the dead man. About the same height and weight and age, and the clothes the man had on were the kind he wore. Besides that, there was one fact that seemed to clinch it. The night before the body was found, Simon Farley was driving home from work about three in the morning. Just as his headlights swept the crown of the bridge, he said, he saw someone jump or fall from the railing. He stopped and ran over to the spot but couldn't make out a thing in the dark. When anyone raised a question, he would say, "Damnit, a fella ought to know what he sees, hadn't he?"

Not always, she would think, especially after the sheriff asked her to go down and identify the body. She told him that from what she'd heard there wasn't much to identify, but she went anyway to help him out and because it was something she would want done for her, if it ever came to that.

She was scared as they entered the chilly room, until the sheriff pulled the sheet back from an ugly and distorted human shape that, as far as she was concerned, was beyond recognition. And the clothes were so torn and filled with silt that she couldn't even identify them for sure.

She had never been convinced that it was him. For one thing, when someone pressed him, Simon Farley always backed down. "Well, you know, a fella's tired that time of the morning and it was dark and anyway who's ever on the lookout for somebody jumping from the bridge every time they go across it?"

More than anything else, though, was what John Jacobs himself had said about the river, at times when he had been truly serious with her.

He had described to her how late one night—maybe even from the bridge—he had watched the current and waves capture and twist and weave long strands of light like taffy, pulling them downstream until they came together as a thin thread that finally disappeared. Or there was the afternoon he had sat listening to tongues of water lapping the bank and how, since it was quiet and he was able to concentrate, he had heard the deep water moving, like the sound of a long, drawn out sigh. The river was unstoppable, he told her. No matter how many dams were built, it would still reach the ocean and from there would come back as rain to feed itself. It was an unbreakable cycle. If she really wanted to learn about the river, he said to her, she should read Huckleberry Finn. Then she would know what he was trying to say.

She understood enough to see how much he loved the river, and feared it, too—maybe respected was a better word—and she kept it all to herself. It didn't concern anybody but him and her, and remembering his words made her feel better. A person who said things like that wasn't just going to up and do himself in. He wasn't the kind. It was more a case of him being plain too antsy to stay in one place forever. She was sure, now that she'd mulled it over a while, that he had finally gotten rested up—he had come there to rest; he'd said so himself—and just left without telling anybody, even her. He was at that very minute—she knew it as well as her own name—sitting in another bar in another town making small talk to the bartender.

She heard them coming. Straightening her apron, she lined up a row of glasses and positioned herself behind the tap.

"He's a son of a bitch!" George Simpson said to another man as they crashed through the door. George was huge with the still-firm fat of youth, a pack of cigarettes rolled up in a sleeve of his stained t-shirt. "And I've about had it with him." He pivoted a quarter turn at the counter and said, without changing his tone of voice, "Hello, Estelle, baby. How about a pitcher and two big ole glasses—and a kiss, too, if you can spare one."

"All used up today," she said, smiling and thumping the pitcher down.

"Too bad."

She brushed his hand away from her cheek and filled a glass.

"Because if he doesn't leave me alone, I'm going to smash his goddamn face in," George was saying as he and the other man stomped toward a booth.

So it began. Glasses and pitchers went out full and came back empty. Soon all seats were taken and late-comers wandered from place to place, stopping to chat, moving on, everybody getting louder and louder as they tried to be heard above the noise.

Like clockwork, she thought, and it was her business to keep the parts going, as she had been for nearly twenty-five years.

Then, from somewhere, she didn't see who had done it, a fifty-cent piece slid toward her. She ignored it and went on smiling and bartending. But before long she found herself peering over the shoulders of customers at the counter and glancing, when she had a chance, at the front windows. She shook her head. Such damn foolishness.

Gary D. Wilson

Winter Solstice

For nearly an hour he had banged doors, cursed, thumped boxes on the floor above her, but not once had he yelled, "Ada, where is—?" to interrupt the furious crocheting she started whenever he was out of the room.

The afghan was a Christmas present for their daughter. She would have to crochet straight through to finish, which was impossible because he never gave her peace. If she tried to work in front of him, he would pucker his lips and mince pinched fingers to mock her until she surrendered and put the yarn away. But for some reason that afternoon he had pushed himself up and shuffled toward the stairs, the first time in days he had been out of his chair except to go to the bathroom or to bed. What he was doing and why didn't concern her. She was pleased to have a few minutes to herself. If she were lucky, he would see fit to slam around for another hour. Maybe two. In fact, she didn't care if he never came down.

"I don't," she said to herself and tensed. But there was no rush of the embarrassed guilt she used to feel when such thoughts crossed her mind. "I really don't," she said aloud, then glanced from side to side to be certain no one had heard her.

She might have felt sorrier for him if he were an invalid, if he truly could do nothing but sit and stare hour after hour, day after day, television shows melting into each other like layers of snow in the spring. Of course he hurt. So did she. They were getting old and hurting was part of that. But his attitude was if he couldn't work the way he had when he was thirty-five, to hell with it. And with her, too. As if it were her fault. As if she were the one who had held up the hope that he would get better.

"I'm not a goddamn mule," he would say. "I know what's going on here."

Then he would pause and, instead of explaining, sink back into his old complaints: "What have I done to deserve this? Why me and not somebody else?"

When she suggested he was fortunate not to be stuck in a wheelchair or bedridden, he would snap: "How would that be any worse than what I'm going through now?" So they didn't discuss it any longer, and in the past few months their conversations had shriveled to petulant remarks and barked commands: Pills. Coffee. Food.

It wasn't that he couldn't take care of himself. He simply refused to. She went along to avoid the storm that would rage if she didn't. She wished now she had never started. The more she did for him, the more crotchety he got, and more often than not hatred sparked from his eyes. Why, she didn't know. If he was unhappy with what she was doing or the way she was doing it, he could change everything with a word. But he hadn't and her resentment grew until the mere sight of him left a bitter taste in her mouth. Every day now she experienced a twinge of excitement, deep in that corner of herself she never showed anybody, at the thought that he was not going to live forever.

A rumbling whump came from directly overhead. She clutched the afghan, wondering if he had fallen, had a heart attack. She couldn't possibly move him, and he might die before she could get help, his face grey, eyes bulging as he clawed the dusty air for a breath.

A grating sound, like a carton being pulled across the floor. She yanked out the last dozen stitches, starting that part of the row again with less tension on the yarn.

She wished she knew what to do. He probably needed her help, but if she went to him, he would get angry because she was there, and once she was finished he would never say Thank you. Good job. Kiss my ear. Anything.

That was because no one could ever say or do enough to satisfy him. Or so Ellen, her youngest sister, had described him during a recent visit. She was pretty and sophisticated and had a way with words that made Ada value her opinions. Ellen said she either had to begin saying no to Henry and damning the consequences—which would make life unpleasant until he saw that regardless how much he pouted and fumed, she wasn't going to back down—or she had to get away from him completely. To do nothing was to let the situation get worse and worse, but neither of them wanted to talk about what that could lead to.

Her sister was right, she supposed. The strain was already beginning to show. Her digestion was terrible. She had violent headaches. Some evenings her heart felt like it would fly out of her chest. Yet she would have put up with any of those to be rid of the sickness that came to her mind. At times she worried that her brain was rotting and were someone to lift off the top of her skull, great billows of green gas would escape, carrying with them her most frightful visions. It was in those moments that she was sorriest for Henry. His brain was probably mush going on gel, and all his thoughts and images were so scrambled they would never make sense.

Hearing him on the stairs, she tucked her yarn into the bag and pretended to watch television.

He groaned down the last step, sighing once both feet were on the floor.

"Did you find what you were looking for?" she said.

He held the small flat box in front of him as he hobbled toward his chair. "Get my cleaning kit."

"Isn't it too cold to work on the car?"

"Christ's sake, woman! The one for my guns."

It might have been the chair or the way he was sitting, but as she went by he seemed more shrunken and pale than ever, fingers with long, curved nails trembling on the box. A strand of cobweb was caught in his hair, hair that was now white and so thin she could see his whole scalp. She reached out to brush the cobweb away, then drew her hand back. He hated to be patted and stroked.

She found the kit under a pile of brown paper bags in the kitchen pantry. Gun oil from the rag inside had soaked through the cardboard lid. She like the clean, fresh smell and held the kit to her face for a moment.

He took it from her with a grunt. Inside was a bottle, a rag, a small screwdriver and a metal rod, each of which he placed on the end table beside him before unfolding the blue felt cloth that covered the gun, a .22 caliber pistol he had bought years ago for her protection. It was a six-shot revolver with a mother-of-pearl handle, so sleek and shiny already it seemed to her more like another piece of furniture than a weapon.

He draped the felt cloth across his lap and slowly took the gun apart, inspecting each screw and spring under the light before laying it aside.

When the gun was new, she'd had to do the same thing. He had insisted that she be able to break it down, clean it and reassemble it, correctly naming all the parts. "You can't learn to use it right until you know how it works," he'd said.

She passed that test and he took her to a grove of trees in the country where he tacked up a paper target. He loaded the pistol and handed it to her. The first shot was surprising. She had expected it to be thunderous, but it was more like the pop of a cork being pulled from a bottle, only leaner and crisper. She stood sideways to the target and lowered the sights to the bull's eye, then under it slightly, back up until the gun was perfectly aligned. She squeezed the trigger, as he'd said, not yanked. A pop, a twitch in her wrist. Six tries, six holes within the circles on the target. From the beginning, she was on the mark, yet she was never convinced that pieces of lead traveling so fast they were invisible made the holes. They looked more like she had stabbed the target with a knitting needle.

"You're all set," he had said. "Aim at the head or the heart. Nobody with any sense will bother you then. If they do—"

"Nobody with any sense," she repeated to herself as she went to the kitchen to fix supper.

She enjoyed cooking, whether he liked what she made or not, because she was alone and could ponder things without him saying, "What's bothering you?"

"Nothing," she would say.

He would stare at the television for a while, watching her out of the corner of his eye, then say, "There is, too, or you wouldn't be so down in the mouth. What is it?"

"Nothing. I'm fine."

"You afraid to tell me?"

"There's nothing to tell."

"You think I might die if I hear about it?"

"Henry, for godsake."

"I'm not a moron. I can see when something's bothering you. Is it one of the kids'?"

"No, it's not them or me or you. I'm just sitting here. Is that all right?"

"You don't have to get snippy."

She would sigh.

He would sigh.

"Why are you badgering me?"

"Why are you badgering me," he would mimic in a high nasal twang.

She would cry.

"Nothing worrying you, huh? Sure looks that way. But that's fine. You don't want to tell me, go on and keep it to yourself. I'm just a sick old castoff son of a bitch anyway."

He would sit back then, becoming more and more pallid as he kneaded the knobs on the arms of his chair. "Get me a pill," he would finally say in a choked voice.

She would, one of the nitroglycerin tablets no bigger than a pinhead, and he would relax as soon as he'd taken it, and she would say, "I'm sorry, Henry, I didn't mean to," without knowing exactly what she was sorry for or what she hadn't meant to do. But he would pout for hours, glaring at her from time to time to be certain she hadn't forgotten.

And he wasn't that way only with her. He treated his family, hers, the neighbors the same. If they wouldn't argue with him so he could be hurt and have their sympathy, they weren't worth a damn. Like Ellen. She had never let him get her goat, and he hated her for it.

Ellen's last night there, the two of them had stayed up and had a long talk after Henry had gone to bed. They sat at the kitchen table and drank coffee and kept their voices low. Ellen thought Henry was acting stranger than ever. She didn't like to think about leaving Ada behind with someone who seemed so unstable. She wanted to know whether Ada felt she could trust

Henry. The idea shocked her. She had never given it a thought until then and concluded that of course she could. He might be cantankerous and peevish and generally hard to get along with, but that didn't mean he was dangerous. Did it?

"Supper's ready," she said, putting the last bowl on the table and seating herself.

She waited a couple of minutes, as usual, watching steam rise from the food. "Henry?"

The cat and mouse game. It was her duty to seek him out.

"Don't blame me if the food's cold," she said, going to the doorway.

"I didn't hear you call," he said too nicely, spinning his chair around. He put the pieces of the gun on the end table and grunted to his feet. "What are we having, corned beef hash?"

"As a matter of fact we are."

He smiled and she didn't know how to take it.

"Amazing. I was just thinking about corned beef hash. Used to have it in the army. I guess cleaning the pistol reminded me. Might have been the cooking smells, too."

He doubled his right leg under him as he lowered himself onto the chair. His circulation was so poor the doctors had warned him not to cross his legs or sit on them, but he did it anyway.

They ate in silence until he raised his fork, turning it prongs down, and waved it, as though to direct her attention.

"There was one time I'll never forget, when I got the riot act read to me in the mess hall. Boot camp, I think it was." In mid-air, the fork flipped to its side, breaking rhythm. "Have I told you this before?"

At a thousand meals. And she didn't want to hear it again, not because the story was too tiresome, but because he was telling it only to torment her, which is exactly what Ellen would have said in no uncertain terms.

"We were sitting there grubbing down and I was talking to this guy next to me when a sergeant comes by. 'What was that I heard you say, soldier?' he yells. I told him and he says, 'How long you been here, soldier?' 'Three weeks,' I say. 'And you still don't know what to call your weapon?' He's screaming now and everybody in the mess hall can hear. 'Well, we have ways to make you remember,' he says, and I just about crapped when he gave me the order. I had to stand on the table, you see, and unzip my fly and take my pecker out and repeat:

This is my rifle, this is my gun.
This is for fighting, this is for fun.

Twenty times, with my rifle in one hand and it in the other. Let me tell you, that was embarrassing. But I learned my lesson. I never got them mixed up after that."

Her head was down, eyes closed. She could feel him staring at her, expecting her to laugh and say, "What a funny story." But this time, no, she wasn't going to.

"One thing for sure," he went on. "They didn't put up with any mollycoddling stuff back then. Men were men in those days and acted like it."

"All right, Henry!"

He squirmed, as though she had doused him with hot coffee. "Jesus! Can't even talk in your own house."

"About something else, fine," she said, restraining herself, frightened by her tone. "But not that."

"What then? Crocheting dainty little doilies? Piss on it!" He shoved his food across the table and stood, leaning on the back of his chair to anchor himself. It tipped and he nearly fell. "Leave me alone!"

She sealed the leftovers and put them in the refrigerator. She washed the dishes, wiped the top of the stove and swept the floor. She carried the trash through powdery sifting snow to the barrel by the alley.

But she was still angry when she joined him in the living room. If she hadn't been, she would never have swung the afghan over her lap and begun unraveling yard after yard of yarn.

Without a word, he cleaned and oiled the gun, reassembling it more slowly than he'd taken it apart. Even he seemed to realize there were circumstances when it was better to leave her be. But her mood didn't keep him from peering at her through the gun barrel as he pretended to see how clean it was, or cocking the hammer and squeezing the trigger with the pistol pointed in her direction, or finally loading the gun—a precise, metallic click sounding with each rotation of the chambers—and placing it purposely on the end table between them.

She refused to look at him the whole while, and after he had finished, he shifted restlessly in his chair, eyes and attention wandering.

"Why don't you start a hobby?" she said, using her advantage to head off any reference to the pistol or any complaints about her crocheting. "Something with your hands. Building models or doing needle point. Lots of men do needle point."

He wrinkled his nose.

"It's better than just sitting around."

She didn't even listen to what he said. She knew it by heart, since they'd had the same conversation before, more often than she cared to remember. Like one of those cartoons where a dog and a cat are running in a circle, whirling faster and faster, coming together in a blur that makes it impossible to tell who's chasing who. She shut out the thought, but it left her empty, the anger she had pushed aside pounding again in her ears.

She crocheted frantically until she noticed a missed stitch several rows back. It was a tiny hole, one nobody else would ever see, but it appeared to her as a yawning chasm.

"How do you stand it?" he said, watching her unravel the yarn again. "You pull out more than you put in."

"I have to. I can't give it to Jean full of mistakes."

"Hell, she's got money," he said. "Let her go buy one. You're driving me nuts."

She glared at him, then dropped her eyes, biting her lip, bruising her finger against the crochet hook. "If it bothers you so much, go to bed."

"All right, by jesus, I will, if you'd rather do that than have my company."

He waited, but she said nothing. He went to the bedroom and returned, a pitiful sight standing before her in his pajamas. When she still said nothing, he tottered to the bathroom and back.

"Goodnight," he said, not to wish her a good night, but to announce it was her last chance to change her mind.

She listened to his groans and the squawk of the bedsprings as he got settled.

On television familiar people were doing and saying familiar things, but none of it caught her interest. She switched off the set and slid into her chair, pulling the afghan across her lap. She didn't intend to work on it. She only wanted to feel its softness and to see it and to know that so far it was perfect.

She laid her head back and let silence flood her like a warm bath. Real silence where nobody expected anything, where that moment was all that made any difference.

Cheeks fluttered in the bedroom. Lips smacked. A snort. A short snore.

Anger boiled back. Her fingers shook as she found the yarn and flew through the pattern faster than ever. Too much tension, she knew, but she didn't dare stop.

A snore blasted the room. As though he had planned it. As though he had gone to sleep thinking, I'll teach her.

She held her palms to her ears but lowered them as soon as she realized he was making her do that, too. A thunderous burst rolled past.

Her eyes fell on the pistol. She looked away.

She wanted somebody there now. To talk to. She wanted anybody. But Henry.

She crocheted, driving the hook like a nail.

Maybe she should call Ellen or one of her kids. But what would they say? Get away? Do something before she got sick, too?

Shivering, she slipped her fingers around the cool mother-of-pearl handle. She had forgotten what the gun felt like and turned it over and over in her hand as she listened. It was quiet. Did that mean he was also listening, waiting in the darkened bedroom for some sign that would tell him what she was going to do?

Then the snores were back. Booming. Quaking.

She dumped the pistol into the box and taped the lid shut. Tucking it and the cleaning kit under her arm, she went to the stairway. The door stuck, jiggled open. He slept on.

Upstairs, in the middle bedroom where he had been earlier, she slid the boxes behind a bag of old yarn on top of the dresser. It would be a long while before he found them there.

She felt like a thief, pressing her back to the wall, easing herself down from step to step. The last one gave her away.

"Ada? Ada, where are you?"

She hurried into the living room.

"What were you doing?" He righted himself on the edge of the bed, covers stuffed under his chin.

"Nothing," she said. "Why?"

His eyes stopped at the end table where the gun had been.

"Is something wrong?" she said.

His gaze drifted slowly back to her, and they stared at each other across the dim bedroom.

"No," he said. "I was just wondering."

"Well, everything's fine," she said. "You can go on back to sleep now. I'll be right out here watching television if you need me."

Habits Not Easily Broken

He wakes at six fifteen, even though there's no reason he should other than it's the time he's gotten up for almost thirty years. He's not going anywhere—not right away at least—and he's not expecting anybody.

He sits on the edge of the bed and lights a cigarette, sucks the smoke deep down inside, holds it. Closes his eyes and savors the rush.

On his way to the bathroom he switches on the TV but doesn't stay to watch. It's more for the sound than anything else. The companionship. Smoking on the toilet, he listens to someone talking about rebels somewhere doing something. An ad follows. Sometimes he can't tell which is which.

He finishes the cigarette, flushes, washes his hands and face, tries to decide whether to shave. He did yesterday so he doesn't look all that bad, and he's been thinking about growing a beard anyway. Except it's summer and he would probably itch to death.

Now it's the weather. He steps out of the bathroom to see. Hot. All the way up the plains, clear into Canada. Ninety to a hundred. He wonders how people there take such heat when they're not used to it. How they keep cool. He's thought about moving, starting over somewhere new.

Chance of thunderstorms late afternoon and evening. More of the same tomorrow.

In the kitchen he fills a saucepan half full of water and puts it on the stove. Measures two teaspoons of instant coffee into a mug, one of Coffee mate. He shakes another cigarette from the pack, lights it, rubs his chin with his fingers as he waits. When little bubbles form on the bottom of the pan, he picks it up and swishes the water around. It hisses against the hot metal. He pours it into the mug and stirs.

He sits on the couch inhaling the fumes before drinking. He's always done that. It smells good, feels good, clears his head.

The Royals won last night five to nothing against the Yankees. Another big game for Jackson—a homer and three r.b.i. Maybe he can do both after all. But that doesn't seem fair somehow when there are people who can't even do one thing well. The game wasn't on TV, so he tried to stay up and listen to it. He got to the bottom of the fourth and just couldn't do it anymore and went to bed. He's been going earlier and earlier. One night his brother called from the east coast and found him in bed at eight thirty. What the hell was going on, he wanted to know. Was he drunk or sick or something? Didn't he have anything better to do? Why didn't he read a book, for chrissake, or go out to a movie, something? And what about during the day? What did he do then? Lie around, sit around? What? Did he take a paper? One that had good want ads? Every morning he should be spreading it out on the table, looking for anything that seemed decent, going out and talking to people, acting interested. That's how he was going to make it. He needed to set up a schedule and stick to it. Keep going, keep busy, keep doing.

Maybe he should shave after all.

He wets his face, squirts lather onto his fingers. Menthol. He works it into his beard, picks up his razor. Stops.

Why always the right side first? Why never the left? As far as that's concerned, why does he always put his right leg into his pants first? Why does he wipe himself with his right hand, sleep on his right side, sit to the right on the couch? Why does he do any of the things the way he does them? He moves the razor to his left sideburn. It feels so awkward he's sure he'll cut himself. Not because of the position, but the thought of doing that side first, nothing more, and for a moment he just stands there staring at himself in the mirror, wondering how the hell things ever got to such a point.

He dresses in clean clothes. Jeans, a plaid short sleeve shirt. That's all he ever wears. Cowboy boots.

By seven thirty he's ready and even though he's not hungry, he drives downtown to the cafe where he knows Fran will be on the lookout for him.

She named it the Corner Cafe because it's located on the corner of Main and First Streets in an old bank building. A strange place, he thinks, since you have to climb probably ten or twelve steps—he's never actually counted them—to the door, big bumpy limestone walls rising in front of you, up and up and up until you're surrounded by them, both sides and over your head, heavy and solid and not one bit inviting. He saw a picture once of a tomb over in Greece or someplace and that's what it reminds him of walking up there. He should tell Fran that. She'd have a hissy, say tomb my ass. See anybody dead in here?

"Well look what the cat's drug in," she calls out from behind the counter, glancing at him, the clock. "I was about to send old Hank here to come looking."

Hank pushes back his police hat and tips his head to one side, like he thinks that would be a big deal or something. Smirks a little but can't hold the pose longer than a few seconds and looks back down at the table, stirs his coffee.

There are several other people scattered here and there and he greets them as he makes his way to the counter. They wave and nod. A couple call out, "Hey, Hooter, how you doing?"

His real name is Albert. Albert Dawes. People call him Hooter because of the way he laughs—Hoo Hoo Hoo—like a damn old hoot owl, somebody once said, only quieter. But there's nothing he can do about it any more than he can the way he looks. His father did it and his grandfather before him. Maybe even his great grandfather, but nobody knows for sure about that.

He swings his leg over the stool and sits down. The same stool as always. Third from the end. The right end, he's thinking as Fran sets his breakfast in front of him. Eggs sunny side up, bacon, hashbrowns and toast. Day in and day out, except for Sundays, when she's not open.

"You don't look so good," she says. "What's the matter?"

"Nothing. Just been thinking is all."

"That's enough to make anybody sick."

"I suppose. Do too much of it anyway."

"So what about?"

"What?"

"You said you been thinking. What you been thinking about?"

"Things."

"Jesus, man, what kind of answer is that?"

"Not much of one, I guess."

"All right, you don't want to talk, fine. I got plenty of other things to do."

He watches her as she makes rounds with the coffee pot. The way she walks, pushing up on her toes, sort of, with each step and twisting just a little. Gives her hips a nice sway. Not sassy, but smart, and he likes to think she puts it on just a tad bit more for him.

"Why don't you run away with me?" he asks when she steps back behind the counter.

"And you think you got troubles now?"

"Be worth it. Come on."

It's a game they play fairly often. When she's in the mood, she goes along with it. When she's not, she walks away.

"Where do you have in mind this time?" she says.

"It's up to you."

"Mexico then. I've always wanted to go there."

"I don't speak the language and I hear you can't drink the water."

"To hell with water."

"All right," he says, "Mexico it is."

"Say, Fran," somebody calls out, "you saving any of that for us or does old Hooter get it all?"

"Don't worry," she smiles. "There's plenty to go around." And she's off again, refilling coffee, delivering orders.

He finishes eating, has a cigarette. She bustles about a little more then brings the coffee pot by him.

"Just one problem," she says.

"What's that?"

"You got any idea what we'd live on?"

"Love."

She breaks into a huge grin. "I hear tell you can get mighty damn skinny doing that." Picks up his plate and pushes backwards through the swinging door into the kitchen.

He's glad he came now. Always is once he's seen her. If it wasn't for old Fred back there cooking, he'd probably do more than just kid around. Maybe even take her out or something. Try to at least. And say he did. Say they went out a lot and

Fred dropped dead or something and they got married. They'd have a blast. Wouldn't be anything to stop them, would there?

"More coffee before you go?" she asks. "Hooter?"

Fran's holding the pot toward his cup.

"No thanks, I've had enough."

She sets the pot down. "Thinking again?"

"Yeah, I guess. Must have been."

"You look so sad. Tears me up."

"Why don't you do something about it then?" he says.

"You know, I just might, if I really thought I could. But nobody can. Except you. You can do something about it. You could get the hell out of this town for one thing. There's nothing holding you here. You got no mama or daddy, no wife now either, and your kids are off on their own. What is it? What's keeping you? You don't even have a job anymore, for chrissake. This hand to mouth business is okay for a while, but you can't live like that the rest of your life."

"I've got a little put away. From the folks."

"But you'll use that up soon enough. You wait. Then what? What if you get sick or something? What if something happens to you?" She looks down, away toward the far reaches of the room. "I'm sorry, I got no business saying things like that. It's your life. You gotta do what you gotta do. Only I just wish—"

"Yeah?" The metal ashtray pings as he taps his cigarette against it.

"Nothing."

"Come on, what?"

"I just wish you could be happier is all."

Nobody's ever said that to him in his whole life. Nobody. He has to turn away, look at the cigarette machine like he's studying it, like he's trying to decide whether to kick the son of a bitch in or not, his eyes filling with tears. Because what he'd like is he'd like to grab her and hug her and cry. Cry like a little baby or a big baby, it doesn't matter, just cry because it seems like it'd feel so good. But it's not the time or the place and he clears his throat and reaches over for a piece of the newspaper and holds it in front of him. Doesn't read it but holds it until she goes away.

Everything's back to normal when he's ready to leave. She meets him at the register. He pulls out his wallet. She tells him the meal is on the house. He says he can't do that and she says it's her place and she can do any damn thing she wants to. He shoves five dollars onto the counter. She hesitates, takes it, rings up the sale and asks what he's got going today. He shrugs and she tells him to drop back by at dinner and supper time, if nothing comes up. They could use the help. He says he'll see. And thanks.

There are a few cars on Main Street, generally coming into town. To the grocery store, the feed store, the hardware, though it's half antiques now. Hard to find a screw in there sometimes. If he had the money he could start a store himself. A general store, sell a little bit of everything. Clothes, hardware, tools, you name it. Be like nothing else here, only so many people have gotten out of the habit of buying in town he's not sure it would work. Everybody heads over to Newton to the big discount stores or down to Wichita to the malls.

He drives north toward the highway, stops in at the Quick Pik for cigarettes. Nobody there he knows. Some kid behind the counter talking to her boyfriend on the phone. Sounds like they're arguing. He leaves as soon as he gets his change, even though he likes to hang around sometimes for the air conditioning.

A half mile west he stops at the bait shop. Nobody's there but Fat Louisa who laughs all the time. It's annoying and he doesn't like being alone with her. She must be crazy. A little bit at least. Say hello and she'll laugh. Goodbye. Kiss my ass. Doesn't make any difference. Open your mouth and she's already grinning. He doesn't see why Merrill keeps her on, except she's steady and she gets her work done and that may be about all you can really ask of a person.

He pumps a couple dollars' worth of gas at the Co-op, enough to get him by the next day or two no more than he's been driving. Used to be with a round trip to work at the trailer factory in Newton every day he'd take a tank or two a week. Sam, the manager, kept a regular account in his name. He'd gas up and go, pay at the end of the month. Not now. Now Sam takes his money and ducks back inside without a word.

But that's the way it is everywhere. The grocery store, the bowling alley, Randy's Garage, you name it. People take his money all right, but they act like they're stealing it or something, like they might catch something from it, bad luck or something and it's best to get rid of it as soon as possible. When he was first laid off everybody seemed to have lots of things that needed doing. Hauling this and that, cleaning, repairing, painting and such. Not now. Now it's all dried up. Like maybe he's already done everything that needs doing or it's just too painful or too embarrassing to have him around, since he was one of them not so long ago and who knows, maybe even passing the time of day with him—let alone having him around working—could just possibly, not that anyone actually believes such things in this day and age, but could just possibly bring his woes down on all their houses.

Exhausted—from what, he's not sure—he lies on the couch at home and waits. He drinks a beer, smokes a cigarette.

He reaches out and flicks on the TV. The Cardinals and Astros. He turns it off, drains his beer, drops the cigarette butt in the can and goes to the bathroom.

Maybe a nap, although if he sleeps now he won't be able to tonight. Then everything gets mixed up, turned around even more than it is already.

There's more beer in the icebox, but he doesn't want that. Some cheese. He breaks off a chunk and eats it. Needs something to kill the aftertaste, remembers the bottle of Old Grandad he keeps in the pantry.

A golf match on Channel 12 seems better than nothing.

Around a quarter to five, drunker than he should be at that time of day, he heads back down to the Corner Cafe. The supper rush comes between about five and seven and he wants to be there to help out.

"Getting a little headstart on the evening, are we?" Fran says, watching him struggle into an apron.

"Maybe."

"Well just remember the dishes cost money and keep the water hot."

"Gotcha."

She rolls her eyes and shakes her head.

"M'arright. Really." As if that should end the matter.

She goes out. He appeals to Fred. "Am, goddamnit. Look." Holds out his hand. "Steady as a goddamn rock."

"Don't forget these pans," Fred says.

He stays late, helps clean up out front too. Wipes down the tables and chairs, booths and counter, turns the chairs upside down and stacks them on the tables. While he sweeps and mops,

Fran refills salt and pepper shakers, napkin holders. Fred cleans the grill and kitchen floor, then says he's had it, he has to get the hell out of there. Fran pats him on the cheek and says, "Such a sweetheart." Fred pats her on the rear and says he'll see her later.

She goes back to work, and Hooter tries to, but it's harder now with Fred gone, since he can't take his eyes off her. Can't get it out of his mind how pretty she looks, how she'd feel, taste, smell, how much she'd probably enjoy it herself, and he sees them in bed, not his mother's, but his. Sees them, hears them breathing, talking in low voices, feels skin touching skin.

"Fran?"

She's ignoring him, he decides, the tone in his voice, as she begins to clear the register. First she runs a total for the day, rips out the tape and sticks it in the bank bag she's holding, takes out the money, except for a dollar's worth of change, being sure to leave the drawer open just so, puts the money in the bag with the tape and zips it shut. Then she stands behind the counter looking around a moment longer, as if making sure she's remembered everything.

"I've been thinking, Fran."

She glances at him, smiles. "Again?"

He can't stand it. Her lips, her nose, even her ears.

"I've been thinking maybe—"

"Maybe what?" she says after a bit, brows raised, the tip of her tongue between her teeth.

"Maybe we. . .you and me. . . ."

She leans across the counter and kisses him. A peck on the cheek, like his mother might, or his Aunt Mary.

He backs away, hand to his face. She might as well have slapped him.

"Listen, I'm sorry, okay? Hooter? Look at me, will you? You're a nice enough guy. You're even cute. But it just wouldn't work. It'd be like putting a band-aid on a hemorrhage, wouldn't it? You need more than a quickie. You want more than that. Think about what it'd be like tomorrow, the day after. That's not what you're looking for, but that's all I could ever give, because even though it may not seem like it sometimes, I really do love Fred. He's all I've got. All I honestly want. Right now anyway."

So what's he supposed to say? What's he supposed to do? Leave? Stay? Kiss her to show her there are no hard feelings?

He shrugs, turns toward the door.

"Don't go away mad," she says.

"But just go away, right?"

"That's up to you."

"I was pretty well finished anyhow."

"Wait." She unzips the money bag, hands him a twenty.

"That's too much."

"You earned it."

He looks for a smile, a twinkle in the eye, anything. It's so damn hard to know how to take her sometimes.

"Just don't spend it all in one place," she says as he opens the door.

"Yeah."

He takes out a cigarette at the top of the steps, lights it, starts down, for some reason counting this time. Twelve. An even dozen. He's not surprised.

Standing on the corner, smoking, he watches cars drive up and down the street. Normally, he'd wait. Stay right there until she came out.

He flips the cigarette butt into the gutter and heads for his pickup. He gets in, rolls down the windows and starts the motor. But then just sits, hands on the wheel, staring down the street and thinking what a goddamn mess everything is and how he can't bear the idea of going back to the house. Not yet anyway.

He puts the truck in gear and swings a U turn in the middle of the street, goes up Main, passes Hank in the police car on his way back toward town, a couple of other people he knows.

At the end of the street, where the highway intersects with it, he looks west in the direction of the Baitshop and east toward nothing in particular.

What the hell, he thinks. What difference does it make where he goes or how long he stays? He can drive all night if he wants to, all day tomorrow. He might even go to Kansas City. It's not that far. Go up and stay over, maybe take in a Royals game, eat at a good steakhouse. He's got enough cash for an emergency, a credit card. There's an all night truckstop at Florence where he can get gas, a six pack and cigarettes. So what's to stop him?

A car pulls up behind him. Bunch of kids. They honk.

"Shit or get off the pot, mister."

"Up yours," he mumbles, pulling across the highway toward the Quick Pik to turn around and head back down.

The Man Who Wanted to Make Things Grow

He hobbles along the stubby hedge that hasn't needed trimming since he planted it twenty years ago. The pain in his legs stops him every few steps as he paces off the far side, pivots haltingly and measures the end nearest me. He hasn't seen me yet, the grey man who counts, multiplies, divides, trying to decide how to fill the empty space.

He wipes his forehead and squints up at the sky. His hand waves in a half-circle above his head, as if signaling for something to descend, and lands, scratching, on his bare scalp. Spitting on the frozen ground, he continues calculating.

His plaid jacket is too light for the weather, as are the corduroy slippers. He hasn't shaved and moisture collects like spilled soup on his chin whiskers.

He lights his pipe and chokes on the smoke, face graining, lips deepening to dark purple. "So that's what I'm going to do, Bud," he says, as though he expected me to be there, never to have left his side. "I'm going to build me a greenhouse right here." He swings his arm around the little plot and smiles. "According to my measurements, this is forty-four feet, ten inches by twenty-three feet, six inches. Taken from a three foot, two inch stride. Anyway, it's plenty big enough for what I want." He moves to the center of the rectangle and gazes at the giant elm tree shading the spot. "We'll lay a cement slab first, just inside the hedge. Should have left the one from the barn, but, no, your mother said it wouldn't look nice. No matter. It's done now. Then," his excitement gathering, "then, what I'd really like to do is put up a small geodesic dome. I've been reading about them. Wouldn't be too hard once we got started. We'd have to trim out those branches. The nice thing about a dome is that sunlight comes in from everywhere, not just the top. Things grow better."

Puffs of steam curl around his jaw and neck as he wobbles toward me. His touch is so light I glance down to be certain his hand, chapped and weathered as an old board, is on my sleeve. The hard muscles that once danced at work are shrunken under pale skin that tightens on bones. The fingers can no longer grip my wrist until I wince. The hard eyes and challenging smile, goading me to keep pace, have softened and grown inward.

"You remember that day we started on the barn?" His hand skips on my coat. "Jesus, that thing must have been there a hundred years. Those square nails, some of them rusted clear through. How old were you? Eleven, twelve? I know you saved up your allowance to buy your own hammer and came carrying it out that morning telling me you were ready. You always were that way, Bud, an independent son of a—" The hand glides away to nest in his pocket. "That was some job, though, wasn't it?"

His mind falters at recalling his anger, his impatience. The crowbar he wielded drew the gnarled, screeching nails loose from the studding and the barn boards fell beside me faster and faster, until I could no longer knock the nails out and stack the lumber quickly enough. He stomped down the ladder.

"Hold the goddamn hammer like a man. On the end, not in the middle. Get some power into it. What are you, some kind of pussy?"

"It's my hammer. I'll use it like I want to. If it's not good enough, you can do it yourself."

His eyes reddened as he raised his hand. "No son of mine is going to talk back like that."

"Clarence!" my mother yelled from the kitchen window. "Don't you hit that boy."

His hand crumpled, falling like a quail shot on the wing, and he mounted the ladder, which trembled and clattered from his rage. The boards came off in splinters and half chunks, as if hit by a sudden strong wind, his bull neck and arms powering the wood to the ground. The frame, naked beams and two by fours, creaked and strained against the rope we pulled, him taunting me about how I leaned into the rope like a girl afraid of getting her dress dirty. My hands burned as I heaved and we ran with it, the frame leaning, us backing up as fast as we could to keep the line tight, and the timbers coming down through the limbs of the elm like dinosaur bones.

The next day, his anger unabated, he attacked the cement slab, the sledgehammer rearing up, ramming down, the earth rumbling under me, and we carted the pieces to the dump in a small trailer. Finally, he leveled the ground with a rake which cut shallow furrows in the soil.

The barn had been his retreat. On summer nights he used to sit alone in the corn crib and drink, his main form of recreation, as he said. But my mother had insisted that the barn be torn down. It was an eye-sore and was dangerous, she said. Besides, my brothers and sisters and I used to play in the loft, and she was convinced that we would get some dread disease from the pigeon droppings. My father never accepted that explanation. I could tell by the way he looked at her that he felt she was trying to take one more pleasure away from him.

After we had dismantled the barn, my mother sat in her faded velvet chair wagging her foot and rubbing the heels of her hands together, making sounds like a dry pump. "We have to do something to fill in that space back there. It's so empty now. What do you think, Clarence?"

He squinted from behind the paper.

"Maybe you could build a tool shed."

He reached for his bourbon and water. With his corn crib gone, my mother had compromised and said he could have one bottle of whiskey in the house. She never did discover the cache of wine he kept in the flush tank of the toilet. She thought his hemorrhoids were bothering him when he stayed behind the locked door.

There were evenings when his anger and drunkenness would converge and a terrible argument would erupt. My mother would tell him he had no respect for anyone but himself—and very little of that—and he should think of the effect his drinking had on his children. He would say that as long as he provided a living for the household he was entitled to do any damn thing he pleased. My mother would counter, and he again. My brothers and sisters and I listened to the voices grow louder from the top of the stairs, my mother demanding that he get out of the house. He would be welcomed home when he was sober. His final statement was a pane-rattling slam of the door.

When we heard Mother's foot tapping on the kitchen tile, we ran off to bed and waited for her to come to see that we weren't frightened. She would nuzzle us and tuck us in, speaking softly until we went to sleep.

"Well, what do you think?" he says, forehead squirming with grey worms of flesh.

He wants me to give him permission to make plans, to say everything is fine and we can start again.

"I think you should come in and eat lunch."

He waves me away. "You're like an old woman. Go have your damn lunch. Leave me alone."

"The doctor says you should rest."

"To hell with him, too. I want to do something." He shuffles to the far line of hedge, halting by the rust-riddled trash barrel. "I had a heart attack, for chrissake. Am I supposed to stop everything now and die?"

"We want you to get well before you try too much."

"That's what killed your mother, if you want to know. Sitting all day by the window, never going out. Never did know what she was thinking about all that time."

The house that my mother kept spotless now looks like a hermitage. The porcelain cover is down over the stove top, dust-cloaked pans dangling on hooks above it. One soaks in the sink, a thick, heavy crust of char in the bottom. The counter is coated with grit and breadcrumbs. The canisters are empty and metallic smelling.

"When was the last time you had a good meal?"

"Oh, I don't know. I was up to the restaurant a while back." The door clicks open and bottles rattle. "Would you like a little nip while you're getting stuff fixed?"

"Yeah, why not?"

He holds the bottle up to the light from the back door, squinting at the liquor level, and measures precise quantities into shot glasses.

"You know, one thing I always wanted was to have a drink with my boys. There's just something civilized to that, sitting down and having a drink together. But you're the only one who takes the time to stop over."

"They all have their own families," I say, putting a sandwich on a plate.

"That's true enough." His head wags over his glass. "How are they, Bud?"

"I don't know much more than you do. I don't see them either unless we happen to be in the same shop or I run into them on the street. Every so often one of them will call and have me over for dinner." I hand him a plate with a sandwich, cottage cheese and fruit.

"That's not good," he says through a mouthful of food. "You need to keep close touch with family. They're the only ones you can ever really depend on when you need help."

"I suppose so."

"Suppose hell! It's the truth!" A piece of lettuce hangs from the corner of his mouth as he peers across the top of his sandwich.

"Let's eat and not talk, all right?"

I force down each bite, the last one burning back up my throat. I quickly clear my dishes and drink a glass of water.

"Food tastes good," he says, wiping his plate with a wet finger. "Guess I was hungrier than I thought."

"You don't eat like you should—and you drink too much."

"Whiskey keeps me going. Food makes me sleepy. I can't waste time."

"If you don't start taking better care of yourself, I'm going to hire a housekeeper to look after you."

"Only if she's pretty and twenty-five. But that wouldn't do much for a heart condition." He hangs his head. "Okay, bad joke. I didn't mean anything."

"You already said it. No sense apologizing."

"I just didn't think. Your mother would have laughed. She always did."

"Forget it, all right?"

"Bless her heart, she was a good woman. Always had the upper hand in everything. I miss her."

"Will you goddamn knock it off!"

"Okay, okay. No need to blow a gasket."

I carry two cups of hot tea to the living room and he clears a space for them among the clutter of magazines and newspapers on the coffee table. The room is long and dark, the only light coming from the Victorian bay windows near where we sit, but they are partially blocked by rows of shelves lined with red clay pots, all barren except for bunches of dead leaves hanging on brown threads of stem.

"Whew!" He sets the tea down with a thunk. "This stuff's too hot. I'm going to have something cool. Can I fix you anything?"

"No.

"Come on, one more won't hurt anything. Be good for you."

"I'd rather have tea."

His disappointment lifts as he huddles over his drink, eyes reading the shelves. "You remember that forest she had in here, don't you?"

"Of course I do."

He nods, sucking his lips. "It was amazing to watch her. I never knew anybody who had such a way with plants. She'd come in here every day with her yellow watering can and go around to each pot like she was visiting a friend. God, it was fascinating. She'd move the plant a few inches one way, then back, asking it which place it liked best. She'd stand there and stroke the leaves and pat the pot, billing and cooing."

"They grew, though."

"Damn right they did. You know, she only had one plant die the whole time I was here." His voice trailed off. "And that was one she threw at me. When she tried to replant it, it died.

The only other times I saw her cry like that was when you kids were sick."

My mother's eyes were swollen and red, but her voice was cheerful. "There now, is that better?" She adjusted the blankets on my bed. "You shouldn't get chilled. That would only make things worse." She never mentioned the word pneumonia to me. "You already have it bad enough, but the doctor says you'll be all right. So we have to keep you warm." She jiggled the window blind. "Is that too much sun? Not enough? You do need some sun. There, how's that?" She sat on the edge of the bed and brushed my hair back. "You'll have to be more careful from now on and stay out of that old barn with those cold drafts and that nasty bird dirt. That's where you got sick, I know it. I tried to tell your father it was no place for you children to play." She sighed. "Well, you sleep now and call me if you need anything. I'll be listening." She went out so softly I wasn't sure she had really been there.

"They're all gone now," he says, the drink nearly finished. "After she died, I tried to keep them alive. I did everything— watered them, sprayed them, even talked to them. They just kept withering up and drooping over. That vine she had by the door was the last. More of it to die, I guess." He shrugs and turns the glass in its puddle of water.

I scoot to the front of my chair. "I have a meeting at two-thirty, and there are some things I need to do to get ready for it, so—"

He cups a strapless wristwatch in his palm. "You have a couple of minutes yet. Sit back down, there's something I want to talk to you about."

I lean my haunches into the arm of the chair, half facing the door.

He stares into the watered remains of his drink. "How much rent are you paying on that apartment you have?"

"Two-fifty, why?"

"That's a lot of money for a teacher. Anyway. I've been thinking lately that, well, it might be nice for both of us if you moved in here with me. Not exactly with me. You could have the whole upstairs to yourself. It wouldn't be hard to put in a bathroom and we could even make an outside entrance for you so you'd have all the privacy you wanted. I mean, hell, we're both sort of bachelors now. And I promise not to listen if you have company over. We could even seal off the stairway." He laughs. "How would that be? And all you'd have to pay is maybe half the utilities or something. We could work that out to suit you. What do you think? A good idea?"

"I really have to get going."

"What the hell makes you so stubborn! Here I'm offering you a deal to help you save a little money. You won't have to worry about me coming up to sit on your lap every day, I can tell you that. So what is it? Why won't you even talk about it?"

I edge toward the door. "I have my own life to live now, that's all."

"No, I know what's going on here. It's let the old bastard rot in the nest he's made. And there may be something to that. But let me tell you, I'm trying, Bud. Goddamnit, I'm trying, if you'll give me a chance."

He follows me to the door with his hand raised. I linger looking back from the front steps.

"Think about it," he says.

The next morning I stop at the plot where he wants to put the greenhouse. A shallow trench has been ripped out along the hedge. Clods form a dull dotted line beside it and icicles flow into a thin sheet of ice in the bottom. The trench ends abruptly ten feet from completion, the pick handle hanging in mid-air, its point buried in the ground.

The house is quiet. I can hear him waiting, not breathing, not blinking, not swallowing against the grape of a cough hanging in his throat. He is on his cot at the far side of the parlor, feet erecting one end of an old army blanket which drops away over the thinness of his body. His bald head, supported by double pillows, is twisted toward the window. Within reach are a small dark vial of pills and a bottle of whiskey.

"Hello, Son." Morning light rolls from his slaty skin. "I knew you'd come."

"Why couldn't you wait until the ground thawed?"

"I wanted to get started." His voice is faint.

"It was a stupid thing to do. If Henry hadn't seen you when he came for the garbage, you'd have frozen to death."

"I wanted to get the footing dug so when it got warm enough we could lay that slab first thing." He raises himself and cocks his elbow against the cot.

"I can't even leave you alone one afternoon."

"Once the slab's down, it's easy. We put up the frame and fit the panels."

"I don't know what I'm going to do with you. I can't spend all my time here."

"Then, by god, we can grow whatever we want to."

"Why are you doing this to me?" I look for a place to sit, away from the sour air surrounding him, but there is none.

"Tomatoes year-round. Mums and marigolds. And house plants."

"You knew how damn sick you were, but there you went anyway."

"We'll take these pots out of here and put them in the greenhouse."

"I think you're trying to kill yourself," I say.

Wincing, he lies back on the pillows, nostrils flared, purple lips parted. "You don't want me to finish it, do you?"

"That has nothing to do with it."

"Yes it does," he says. "Because if it gets finished, that means you and me. Like it was on the barn. We did that and we can do this. Nobody else is going to help me, Bud, that's clear enough."

"I can't, either."

He continues, as if he hasn't heard me, as if he has been rehearsing all night what he is saying. "We've always understood each other. Sure, we've had our fights, but they don't last long. In the end we're back together. You and me."

"I said, I can't do it, either."

His forehead darkens. But he doesn't frown. "Just remember, it's something your mother would have enjoyed. I want to do it for her sake, too."

"Leave her out of this."

"Why?" he says, eyes tightening. "She's been in it all along."

"You won't stop at anything, will you?"

"It's the truth!"

"It's cheap and you know it!"

His chest arches, then folds, as though someone has struck him in the stomach, and he collapses against the pillows, stare riveted to the ceiling, neck corded, chin jutted. His fish mouth chews the air, bubbles of sweat glistening on his upper lip.

He pats the nightstand, searching for the pills. As he unscrews the cap, the vial springs loose, smacking the floor, the tiny white pills floating across the dark wood under my feet like styrofoam pellets.

"I'll get them!" he gasps, leaning over the edge of the bed, an arm tailing the floor. "Stand back, goddamnit! I can do it myself!"

The arm dangles. His face blues, eyes bulging at my shins.

I hoist him back onto the cot, turning my head from the smell, from the gaping pores on his cheek. He clamps his mouth shut, eyeballs rolling up to white. Pinching his jaw muscles, I force his mouth open and place one pill under his quivering tongue. Then another.

He sinks toward the window. I collect the other pills, picking specks of lint from them, and drop them into the vial. Even from the side, the hardness is there in his face, but for one strip of moisture leading from the corner of his eye.

"She always wanted a greenhouse," he says quietly. "It's the least I can do now."

"All right, for godsake! I'll get somebody out here tomorrow to look at it."

"That isn't what I mean, Bud."

"What then? What the hell is it you want from me?"

He rotates his head slowly until he is gazing directly at me. "I want you to say you'll help me when the time comes. See? There you were, all worried for nothing, because that's all there is to it. That's all I'm asking."

A Place Like Harry's

Imagine first an hourglass. Now a map of Madison, Wisconsin, conforming to its shape. The curves follow the shorelines of two lakes named Mendota and Monona because the city's founder thought they sounded Indian. In the center of the isthmus is the state capitol building. It is impossible to pass from one side of the city to the other without taking note of it. Symbiotically, a street called State connects the capitol to the campus of the university. Together they set the tone of life here: well-planned and well-executed, like the perfect garden.

Think of a fashionable apartment building, northwest of capitol square, bordering an exclusive subdivision. Its front is muted, unobtrusive. Its backside, however, opens in tiers of screened porches to the glassy waters of Lake Mendota. Green glass. Old wavy glass that rolls silently against the shore. Picture there a white boathouse, a weathered pier, twin cottonwoods bent in a shimmering arch.

Look back from the lake to the porches. Third floor, left-hand side, apartment 3-8. Harry Felton lives there. Used to, rather. Harry Felton is dead.

Imagine him on his bed. He is covered with a sheet, arms placed neatly to his sides, head now purplish and bloated declined to the right. An empty brown pill bottle is on the nightstand, a sealed envelope beside it propped against a photograph: black and white, a full-body shot of a middle-aged man with greying hair and a square face shiny-raw from aftershave. He appears to be of average height and weight, dressed in pleated tweed pants and a white shirt with a narrow tie. The clothes have a revived rather than fashion-conscious look. He is smoking a cigarette.

Harry Felton worked as a bureaucrat for the state and had lived in 3-8 since the building was finished in 1961. Thirty-nine years. He has no family and no friends close enough to notice his absence. He never married, although if a letter found in a stack of trash is to be believed, he was once engaged to a Jeanette Wilder of Beaver Dam, Wisconsin.

II

Picture being out on this perfect spring day. Crocuses and early tulips have bloomed. Grass has greened. Trees have leaved. Sailboats skim the lake, birds soaring behind them, then falling like chips of sky to the water. All around, people have emerged, filling parks, beaches, yards, balconies with the urgency of hibernating creatures hungry for light and warmth.

Lou Olsen is not among them. Imagine him in an easy chair in 3-A, his back to the window, the wonderful views because sunlight makes him sneeze. Every spring with the regularity of a new deadline in his doctoral program, he develops an incapacitating hay fever, which, since his adviser suffers from a similar condition each fall, buys him an extra two weeks to complete his work. This season he is grappling with his dissertation proposal, tentatively entitled THE NEW PUEBLOS: APARTMENT DWELLERS IN URBAN AMERICA.

He took the job as manager of his building in order to gain field experience, and for the past three years has carefully and methodically observed the people living there. Recently, he distilled those observations into a theoretical description of how significant communal relationships are formed among residents in multiple-unit housing projects. Although slow in coming, what he has done is good. Potentially so good that even with his adviser's pressure to finish his degree and get on with his life, he wants to take the time to do the best job he can. He could finish by the end of the year, but he wouldn't be happy with his work. He has put too much into the study to watch it simply fade into the stacks of data in Memorial Library. What he is on to is of such importance that he knows all he needs for it to be truly monumental is a good example, a nicely human one, to structure his discussion around. And with time and patience and an eye to the future he is sure he will find it.

It is not difficult to imagine him twenty years hence as a pre-eminent authority in urban anthropology, head of the department at a major university, telling his friends and close student associates over cocktails about how miserable he was as a doctoral candidate and about how he nearly gave up his initial study altogether upon finding one of his subjects dead. He will still shiver and swallow back the thought, then go on to explain how fortunate the discovery was in the end. After all, he wouldn't be where he is today without it, now would he?

But for the moment he is only vaguely aware of a noxious odor in the corridor outside his door and wonders what he should do about it.

Consider his dilemma: in his present condition, he cannot trust his sense of smell enough to judge how serious the problem is. He could call the exterminator, but if he comes and, like last time, finds nothing more unusual than a pile of rotting leaves under the hedge, Lou Olsen will be too embarrassed to turn in yet another unauthorized bill to the owner of the property and will probably pay it himself, a situation he can ill-afford.

Or he could ask one of the other tenants, perhaps Julie in 1-B, whom he has long wanted to consult on other matters but has never had the courage. Unfortunately, if she or any of the other tenants has not yet noticed the smell and he calls attention to it, he might damage his credibility with them and thereby jeopardize the outcome of his study. And it is nothing he can in good conscience ask a friend to do, so he is left with but one alternative: to phone the owner and ask if he wants to tend to the problem himself.

But Justin Foote will not be in. He never is. Two years ago he inherited an estate large enough that its management has kept him more occupied than he cares to be. Soon he hopes to have transferred all decision-making powers except the most major to a competent trustee. It is not an easy task, however, to find someone both trustworthy and capable, so, although he does not work in the conventional sense, he is always busy. And he will continue to be because he will always hire people like Lou Olsen to look after his interests when he knows that their interests lie elsewhere. He will thus create a situation in which he will have to make himself available, regardless of the problem, because of his assumption that no one else can or is inclined to do the job as well as he. Such attention to detail will of course take time from activities he would rather be involved in, and he will enter old age a fussy, cantankerous man who feels cheated and therefore hostile toward those who even suggest that his wealth has been anything less than a loathsome burden.

At present, however, he is still young enough to protect himself from being completely overwhelmed and has daily reserved the period from ten to eleven for jogging and eleven to twelve for tennis. Without fail. But he always showers between. At home. It is a habit he cannot break himself of and one that Lou Olsen remembers.

Imagine, then, Justin Foote running the half mile wooded path to the end of Picnic Point and back, on along the lakeshore through campus. The pounding, the jarring, the slap of rubber soles in a strong, steady rhythm. The crystal lake. The sparkle in Peg Reardon's eye. He sprints the last leg home.

Imagine his disillusionment as he picks up the phone expecting Peg's coy reminder not to be late for their tennis match (which they have agreed from the outset will continue through lunch and into a leisurely afternoon "dessert" at his house) and hears instead Lou Olsen's irritatingly nasal description of a smell of indeterminate origin and intensity in the Sherman Avenue apartment building.

Picture him hurrying through his shower—not even pausing to dry his hair—pulling on his royal blue tennis warmups and racing off.

With exactly three minutes to spare, he throws open the door of the apartment building and stops dead in his tracks.

"Olsen, what in god's name is that?"

III

They are framed against the dark background of Harry Felton's doorway. Justin Foote, left hand on the knob, stretches up and presses an ear close to listen. Lou Olsen, barefoot and lanky in jeans and a t-shirt, bends at the waist, watery eyes squinted, finger poised under his red nose.

He sneezes.

Justin Foote asks for the master key. He turns it in the lock and pushes. They both take a step back.

Think brown. A brown wash over walls, carpet, ceiling, furniture. The only color is in a tattered quilt thrown over the easy chair facing the center of the room—away from the grimy picture window, away from the view everyone pays so handsomely to have. The only light is the faint glimmer from a bowling trophy on top of a bookshelf across the room. And permeating the brown, overriding the acrid odor of stale cigarette smoke, the ripeness of ignored garbage, is the timeless and terrifying smell of death.

Justin Foote gags, points in the direction of Lou Olsen's apartment.

"Sure. Help yourself."

Imagine Lou Olsen alone now, aware of but naturally protected from the full impact of the putrefying body in the bedroom. He moves slowly toward the porch door, eyes reading Harry Felton's remains. A book, a lamp, an ash tray, a worn and rickety telephone stand, no TV. Yet not for some moments does what he is seeing come together as a coherent thought: this is indeed a contemporary tomb, as important in what it can reveal as any that history has thus far surrendered. His colleagues will hear the evolution of the idea again and again—how soon after the tomb notion struck him, things began to make sense: Harry Felton's meticulous preparations for death compared to the abysmal condition of the apartment amounted to a statement, whether conscious or unconscious, about how he saw himself in relation to society at large.

Fresh air barges like an intruder around the porch door. He starts to close it, turning to see if anything has been displaced, and finds Justin Foote, wet washcloth to his mouth, waving it wider still. From the look on his face, he seems little inclined to compromise, and Lou Olsen lets the door go.

A lake breeze bursts past, pulling them in its wake along the filth-decked hallway to Harry Felton's bedroom.

The far window is open a crack, the drawn shade above it tapping hollowly. A luminescent green fly buzzes Harry Felton's body, as if making one last pass, then lifts, circles their heads and lazily joins the flow of air to the screen.

With a glance at the corpse—puffy and distended, skin tight against the liquefying insides—and another at the nightstand, Justin Foote shakes his head and motions them out of the room.

"I'm calling the police."

Imagine the consternation of neighbors in adjoining Maple Bluff at seeing the parking pad in front of the apartment building filled with an ambulance and two patrol cars. No lights or sirens. No commotion at all really as the police set about the business of bagging Harry Felton's remains, collecting evidence, taking statements from Lou Olsen and Justin Foote. It is simply that in the eyes of those in Maple Bluff there are respectable ways to live and to die, none of which Harry Felton chose to follow. He was not rich, nor did he pretend to be. He rarely bought anything new, and in thirty-nine years had traded cars only three times; he lived alone and he died alone, apparently by his own hand. All of which merely reconfirms their contention that apartment dwellers are rootless ne'er-do-wells who would be better off living somewhere else.

Imagine Justin Foote pacing the hallway, so late for his tennis match he will be forced to end his relationship with the only woman he ever seriously considered marrying. He will later blame Harry, then fate, then god as he sinks ever deeper into business and despair.

And imagine Lou Olsen, already feeling a sense of gratitude toward Harry Felton and his timely death that he will never be able to express adequately. On several occasions he will start letters explaining how much Harry has meant to him, only to realize halfway through that there is nobody but Muriel Steiner of Fargo, North Dakota, to send them to.

He is allowed one last look at the suicide note, the contents of which will never be made public. It consists of a single sheet of folded paper with a rubber spider taped next to a yellow happy face with no mouth. Below is his stamped signature: HARRY S. FELTON.

IV

Picture the look of surprise on the face of Muriel Steiner when she receives a letter from the probate court in Dane County, Wisconsin, naming her heir to Harry Felton's estate.

"Harry who?"

She is a second cousin, the only surviving member of his family. A large woman in her early sixties, she makes the long trip to Madison by bus so that she can drive Harry's 1987 Pontiac home. She has trouble remembering what he looks like and feels faintly uneasy taking the car and the balance of his bank accounts—a total of $16,311.23. She also claims a picture of Harry Felton from the nightstand. A memento. Something to remember him by. That is, if nobody else wants it. The rest they can do with as they please.

Lou Olsen assures her that they will.

She worries then that there is something of value she overlooked but does not know how to say as much without seeming suspicious and petty, so packs the Pontiac and starts home.

She will use the car until it dies, too, then set it up on blocks beside her house for her nephew to cannibalize. She will spend Harry's money on an enclosed patio off her kitchen, where at the end of each day she can rest her arthritic hips and peer into the splendor of a North Dakota sunset. She will lose the picture soon after returning home. Her daughter will find it years later in the attic and, exclaiming that it is exactly what she has been looking for, will remove the photograph of Harry Felton and replace it with one of her oldest son.

After seeing Muriel Steiner off, imagine Lou Olsen's excitement at the thought of at last having Harry's place to himself. It is better than a gold mine, more important to his purposes than discovering Tutankhamun's tomb or Agamemnon's grave. Here lived Harry Felton, the most perfect example he has found of failure to thrive in contemporary America, and if he is correct, that failure is directly linked to Harry's inability to adapt to changes in his social milieu. But he needs time to collect the data, bring it all together in some comprehensible fashion. Two weeks and he can be over the top.

"Two days," Justin Foote tells him. "I have painters coming at eight sharp Wednesday morning. I want that place cleaned out and ready to go by then."

"But—"

"Look damnit, I'm running a business, not a think tank," he goes on, assuming already the voice and stance that will come to characterize him as a hard-nosed entrepreneur greatly respected in the financial community.

Picture Lou Olsen at three o'clock Wednesday morning, bent over a long folding table in Harry Felton's living room. He can hear the lake, smell its water. More or less. He has not slept in forty-five hours. He has eaten two sandwiches, a bag of potato chips and four packs of Twinkies. Books, objects pass before his eyes and he mechanically records them in a ledger, later to be sifted through and made sense of. They spin as if on a potter's wheel, now slowly, now more quickly, wavering in and out of focus, dream-like.

He starts, neck stiff, arms tingling, and sees a shadow flit across the wall. Some spot in his vision, a fluttering moth which disappears upon reaching his reflection in the darkly transparent porch window. As he rises, rippled yellow lines of light on the lake stretch through his image. He walks toward and finally past himself onto the porch.

Lou Olsen does not smoke. He never has and never will, yet out there that night he will remember wanting to—or at least having an urge to do something with his hands to punctuate his presence, hold him fast, keep him from simply floating off.

It is perhaps at that moment—he will never be certain when the revelation, as he called it, actually came to him—that the two key factors in the last years of Harry Felton's life fall into place.

Long before his suicide, beginning essentially in the summer of 1994 Harry Felton, for all intents and purposes, ceased living. He stopped reading, stopped eating, stopped going out. He developed hypertension and a heart condition, despite which he continued to smoke cigarettes by the carton and drink beer by the case. But alone. Always alone now. He became so reclusive, in fact, that the paint seal left on the porch windows and door when the apartment building was repainted that same summer is not broken until the day his body is found.

At the center of his decline stands Jeanette Wilder. It is her name that appears on an insurance policy issued in 1992 and allowed to lapse in 1994, her name on the package of new black lace underwear in his top drawer, receipt dated May 28, 1994, her name in a set of books on neoclassical English drama. It is her name on the letter dated June 12, 1994—but evidently never mailed—in which she is denounced as fickle, unfaithful and destructive, and is told that as far as he, the writer (presumably Harry Felton), is concerned their engagement is off. It is under her name that an old phone number in Beaver Dam is marked out and a new one in Sacramento, California, is entered.

She is the linchpin, the link between him and the world. To understand anything about Harry Felton, it is necessary to come to grips with her, a woman as elusive as the air itself. And standing in the chilly pre-dawn, sensing things he has no right nor reason to, he realizes suddenly the futility of ever trying to find her.

If he calls the number in Beaver Dam, for instance, he will arouse someone who will claim never to have heard the name Jeanette Wilder, although there will be a woman's voice in the background asking who it is and what he wants, but still not the woman he seeks.

In Sacramento he will talk to a roommate who will say that the Jeanette she knows—and has known for years—is a native Californian who has never lived out of state and has never mentioned a man named Harry. And, no, she is not available for questioning. She is at work.

Or she is recuperating from a serious illness and is not to be bothered.

Or she has married.

Or she has emigrated to Australia.

She is not there—nor here—and never has been. Jeanette Wilder, Lou Olsen finally comes to understand, existed only in Harry Felton's head, as she now exists in his.

For Harry, in the summer of 1994, she came apart. He could see her seams, the fabric of her manufacture. He became disillusioned and cast her aside. But with that act, a new awareness grew: if she, as real as she had seemed, were a mere imaginary being, a creation of his lonely mind, what wasn't? What or who could he ever trust again?

Perhaps Harry Felton stood on the porch where Lou Olsen is now and gazed as he gazes across the lake, with its own tinseled unreality, and wondered as he wonders if that view is only a creation as well, and if one could but set it aside or cut it like a canvas and step through, as Harry Felton must have, what would one see?

An abiding black nothingness. Was that what Harry Felton saw? Is that what Lou Olsen would see if he let himself, instead of shutting his eyes and backing away, returning to his work with renewed, if not frenetic, vigor, finishing all that he has to have done—and more—by the time the painters arrive.

It is a momentum that will continue through the remainder of his degree program and on into the establishment and protection of his career. He will be seen as a bright and energetic scholar, but one whom a few close associates will confide does indeed seem pursued.

At no time in his life, however, will he mention—not to his dearest friend, his wife, anyone—what he experienced early that morning on Harry Felton's porch. The file he will keep on speculations of such nature will be discovered by his wife after his own death. The strange writings will mean nothing to her and she will destroy them.

V

Thursday noon. The painters have gone, Harry Felton's old apartment is back in shape and ready to show.

Imagine Lou Olsen in 3-A, phone in hand, what remains for him to catalogue of Harry's goods stacked in cardboard boxes beside him.

The day is bright, grass and flowers crisply colored, the lake a bed of floating glass. The cottonwoods, the boathouse, the old pier set the scene perfectly.

Justin Foote has told him to emphasize the view when he calls. The view is what sells the place.

"I want to run an ad for three days," he says, "Sunday included, to read: 'Available June 15, one bedroom apartment. Screened porch. Boathouse. Pier. Beautiful view of Lake Mendota. Sherman Avenue. Lease. Security deposit.'"

"No, no price."

Gary D. Wilson

The Unpredictability of Kansas Winters

Next to death and love, men talk most of snow.
Triptych*, **James Bowden*

Bill Ott and Carl Loomis are sitting at the counter in Bertha's, beside each other on stools with red seats and chrome trim, waiting for Willie Norris. He is the night cop, and every morning he stops in at the restaurant to bring them news of the town while they slept. Today he is an hour overdue, a tardiness too great to be explained by the storm.

So they continue to wait, drinking coffee, smoking, eating doughnuts Bertha serves from a plastic pie case.

After refilling their cups, she busies herself along the counter, rearranging clusters of napkin holders, metal ashtrays, salt and pepper shakers, tucking menus in behind with daily specials paper clipped to the outside. Then she wipes off the milk machine and coffee maker. She cleans the stainless-steel ledge on the service window and spins the empty order carousel above it. Finally she sighs, hangs the cloth on a hook and leans against the counter.

The men turn to gaze with her, out over the parking lot, the highway, the school with its sandblasted brick walls and sign that reads:

HOME OF THE BARTLETT'S JUNCTION BRAVES
CLASS B FOOTBALL CHAMPIONS
1963, 1971, 1977

And they continue to stare, as though the act itself might make him appear from the hypnotic snow which drifts softly, quietly past the windows. Lulled, they hardly seem to notice the flakes catch, pause in mid-flight, then swirl and pitch into a frenzied white world.

The gust dies in a long, trailing moan. The snow again floats silently by. They can again make out the parking lot, the highway, the school; and Willie Norris is still nowhere in sight.

He locked the door to the city building and crossed the street to the patrol car. Snow billowed up and around him and blew into the branches of the elm tree on the library grounds, where a few hours earlier a half moon had shown through. But clouds had closed off the sky and begun to settle, first as sleet, then as a fine white powder that sifted over houses and lawns like confectioner's sugar. The real snow had followed, pouring past streetlights into drifts behind bushes and trees and along patches of pavement swept clean by the wind.

He stood a moment longer, looking at the bare bulb above the door he had come out of, hoping to see it flash so he could go back in and pick up the phone and hear Louise tell him it was all a mistake, Joe Freeman was not dead. And he could sit down with a cigarette and a hot cup of coffee, warm and cozy by his little stove until dawn.

But that was not how it was meant to be.

He put the car in gear, and drove up Main Street toward the highway, eyes scanning side streets and houses as he went. After so many years he had seen just about everything: wrecks, suicides, beatings; family squabbles; dead parents, husbands, wives, children. He liked to think there wasn't much left that could bother him. But people acting stupid still did, he had to admit it. People acting stupid when they knew better.

He tapped the brake pedal to keep from skidding. A semi roared by on the highway in front of him. He pulled out and followed until he lost the running lights in the snow squall kicked up behind the trailer. He wondered how far the driver would get before he ended up jackknifed in a ditch.

Miles meant money, so that risk was easy to understand. What Joe Freeman had been looking to gain was not. At forty-three he already had everything others could only dream of. His wife was so smart and beautiful and good everybody loved her. Both of his boys started on the football team, and they were top students, too, a couple of the best kids around. And Joe himself was the most successful lawyer in the county. He knew his business and was reliable and people liked him. It was rumored that he had been asked to run for the state senate in the next election.

So it was just plain dumb for him to be out at Louise's in the first place. Sure, she was pretty and smart, too, in her own way, and with Junior gone now, she was living in that big house all alone, he understood that. But Joe wasn't going to find anything there he didn't have at home, except maybe a quick thrill, which was about the worst excuse Willie could think of. Joe Freeman owed people a better death than that.

He turned north on the county road just past the bait shop. Ahead of him snow swept over flat fields, up over drifts near fence lines and down, forming fine, sharp points that reached across the asphalt like white claws. He drove carefully, picking his way along the two and a half miles to the farm.

A mailbox fastened to a wagon wheel marked the edge of the drive. Buildings appeared bleak and deserted, outlines only, walls with stark black window holes, shadows etched into the snow.

She met him at the door dressed in a long blue robe with lace trim at the neck and sleeves, blonde pigtails hanging like ropes over her shoulders. Her eyes were red and puffy, and her hand trembled on the knob.

A small lamp was on in the kitchen. Near it were a tumbler, a bottle of Seagram's and a pack of Kents. He helped himself to a cigarette while she paced back and forth, arms wrapped about her, saying, "Christ, Willie, he died right there. Christ!" Which must have meant on her, in her. He wanted her to talk, explain what the hell was going on, why people risked everything like that, why they made each other miserable instead of happy, why he gave a damn. But she wasn't going to.

"Where is he?" he said, mashing the cigarette into the ashtray.

Joe Freeman's head was tilted back slightly on the pillow, mouth and eyes open. One arm lay over his chest on top of the sheet, the other hanging out beyond the edge of the bed, palm turned up toward the window. His legs were parted in a shallow V, sheet furrowed between them, swelling over pubic hair and penis. He was grey, blending with the barnyard light, the night, and he looked old. Old and silent as stone.

Louise's voice was grating. "What are we going to do?"

His head snapped around, words already in his mouth, but she seemed so old now, too, and so lonely that he could not bring himself to tell her she should have thought of that sooner. It was over and he needed her help.

"Joe Freeman died in his office, working. You got that?"

She looked at him, but he wasn't sure she saw him.

154

"Do you understand me?"

She nodded slowly.

"Repeat it. What I said."

She did, her voice barely audible.

Good. Now where are his clothes?"

She glanced toward the corner, confused. He had folded and stacked his pants and shirt in an easy chair, socks laid neatly over his shoes on the floor, as if he had been packing a suitcase.

"Give them to me," Willie said, propping the body against him. "We have to hurry before he gets any stiffer."

She stood beside him like a maid with a pile of fresh linen. Willie put on the undershirt, then peeled the sheet down to the foot of the bed.

"Lift his legs," he said, fumbling the jockey shorts around an ankle.

"Shouldn't we at least—" She swallowed, took a deep breath. "—wash him or something?"

"This has to look as real as we can make it. Dead people are dirty."

She held on, head turned, until they were finished.

"Now you get dressed," he said.

She froze, hands pulled away from her sides, fingers spread, staring at the body.

"Look, you're going to have to drive his car to town and help me with him when we get there. So move it!"

When she was ready, they carried the body out. Her face was as dead as Joe's.

"You got gloves?" he said.

She nodded.

"All right, put them on. We only want his fingerprints on the wheel. Follow me. Stay close. And for godsake, be careful."

A white froth of snow boiled between them, the headlights of Joe's car jiggling in and out of view in the mirror. He imagined her ramrod straight, arms locked to the wheel, afraid to turn and look behind her. How quickly it could all change from passion to fear, from being alive to being dead. He was doing the right thing.

He skirted the east edge of town and approached Joe's office from the south, which took them through only two blocks of the business area. There was less exposure that way, less chance of being seen. They parked in the alley, kept free of snow by the wind. Willie pried open a window and unlocked the back door from inside. They toted the body down a short hallway to the office where Willie sat Joe in the desk chair, then slumped him forward, arranging one arm so that it reached toward a picture of Margaret and the boys. He overturned a coffee cup, blew ashes out of the ashtray, fixed the feet and legs, and stood away with his hand to his mouth, like a movie director.

"Anything else?" he said. "Oh, hell yes."

He hurried to the bathroom, relieved at the sight of hand sanitizer. He grabbed it and a wad of paper towels and swabbed out the back seat of Joe's car, leaving the door open a bit to air out the fumes.

She stood shivering beside the desk.

"Okay. Let's go."

He drove her back to the farm and they sat in the driveway not talking, like teenagers who'd had an argument. He leaned against the steering wheel, chin resting on top of it. She had one leg out of the car but didn't seem ready to go. When he finally spoke, it was as if he were reciting a list of her faults.

"Burn those sheets," he said. "Turn the mattress, too, if it's in bad shape. You hear me?"

Her pigtails jerked up and down as she nodded.

"Get rid of anything that was his. It's hard enough the way it is, and we don't want to have to answer a bunch of questions."

"I'm scared, Willie."

"So am I. If you can think of a better way to do this, shoot."

He waited until a light came on inside the house before starting back to town.

At Joe's office he called Doc Marley, then sat in one of the client's chairs and smoked a cigarette, eyes roaming the diplomas and certificates on the wall behind the desk, the shelves with the heavy dark law books he had always been curious to look at. Now he would probably never get the chance. He glanced at Joe Freeman. He hadn't thought about it in terms of never, but that was what it was all about, wasn't it? Never.

He jumped up and walked to the back door, wishing the hell Doc would come on.

But Doc had stopped hurrying years ago. Even when he got there he took his time, setting down his bag, hanging up his coat and hat, cleaning his glasses. Then he made one complete circle of the body before stooping to examine it more closely. He brushed at a dust smear on the left leg, sniffed the shirt, pinched the skin on the arm. He righted the coffee cup and tipped it over again. He tested a wrist joint for stiffness, studied the fingernails. He eyed the angle of the chair and body in it.

He straightened, shaking his head, then bent over again to get a better view of the face and stood there a long while, as if expecting Joe Freeman to explain.

"Pretty strange," he said, wiping his hands on a red and white bandanna. "But that's all I can do here. I'll get Millard over to pick up the body. Soon as I'm through, I'll give you a ring."

It was five-thirty when he called Willie at the city building.

"I saw what I needed to," he said. "You can put 'apparent heart failure' on your report. 'No evidence of foul play.'"

By six Willie was on his way to the angular green ranch-style house near the park. A nightlight was still on in the hall and he had to knock twice to rouse Margaret Freeman.

She leaned against the door frame, hugging herself, eyes fixed on the snow-covered planter by his feet. Then she seemed to realize who he was and asked him in.

At the kitchen table she sat across from him, still groggy, trying to blink the sleep away. He shifted in the chair and cleared his throat. She glanced up.

"I should at least offer you some coffee."

"No, no," he said. "Don't bother."

But she was already on her way to the sink.

"It looks terrible out there," she said, a tremor in her voice. "I suppose you came all the way over here in this snow to see Joe, but I'm afraid he's—"

There was a swelling in his stomach and chest, a sudden emptiness. He licked his lips and looked down, feeling dry and dirty as old newspaper.

"What is it?" she said. "What's wrong?"

He coughed again. It was a rotten thing. She deserved better, and he wished he knew how to give it to her.

"What-is-wrong?"

"Maybe you ought to sit down."

Her face was pale, mouth open.

"Joe'?"

"Yeah," Willie said.

"What? Tell me!"

"He's dead."

He moved to catch her, to tell her all the things he had thought of—that as terrible as it was she should not give up. In time everything would work itself out. She'd see, it would. But even in his mind the words sounded forced and awkward, as though they had gotten mixed up with his feet and he was about to kick them at her rather than say them. So he stood where he was, turning his hat round and around in his hands, listening helplessly as she sobbed and chanted, "God, oh, god, oh, god, oh, god."

She pushed herself up then and ripped a paper towel from the holder.

"Doc says it looked like a heart attack. I don't think he suffered much."

"No, they never do, do they?" she said to the sink. "I'm sorry. That wasn't very kind of me."

He shrugged that it was all right and patted his pocket for the cigarettes he had left in the car.

"Do you know when—"

"I found him a little after three. At his office," his voice rising despite his efforts to keep it down, and she stared at him as though he had spit tobacco on her floor. "Doc said it couldn't have been a whole lot before that."

She nodded, her finger following the chrome strip between the sink and counter, back and forth around the same corner again and again.

"It's so strange," she said, half to herself. "I knew he was going to be working late and I almost went down to see him. It was just about that time, too. I got up and dressed and was out the door when I thought how silly it was to walk all that way in the snow and went back to bed. If I'd gone on and not let that stop me— The worst thing in the world is to die alone, and maybe I could have—"

"Don't be too hard on yourself," Willie said.

She frowned.

"I mean, there's no guarantee you'd have seen him before—"

"But I might have. I'd have been with him then. When it happened."

"Could be," Willie said. "Except I'm sure this was the best way. Just sure of it."

She still seemed troubled, and he damned himself for not knowing what else to say without making it worse. "Look, I'm sorry as hell about this. I really am. And I'd like to help. If I can call somebody and have them come over and stay with you, or anything like that—"

"No."

"Or I could get you something maybe. Fix you a drink."

She shook her head. "I just need a little time. Alone, before the boys wake up. You understand."

He put his hat on and walked with her to the door.

"Oh, and, Willie—"

"Yeah?"

"Thank you."

Tire tracks lead across Bertha's parking lot to the highway. The right turn signal on the patrol car blinks through exhaust and blowing snow. The rear wheels spin, catch on the pavement, and he is gone.

The men turn back to the counter. Bill strokes his lower lip and stares at his empty cup. Carl scratches the pale scalp under his cap. Bertha winds a dishtowel and pulls it tight between her hands.

"That's the damnedest thing I ever heard," she says, the towel going limp.

"It's something all right," Carl says.

"A hell of a note," Bill says.

"Think about those two boys," Bertha says, "having to grow up without their daddy now."

"Won't be exactly easy for Margaret," Carl says.

"No, but she at least knows what's going on. Them—"

"They ain't babies, for godsake," Bill says.

"It's still a bad age," she says. "Lots of kids have trouble."

"Could be," Carl says, "but her and Joe was awful close."

"Glad I didn't have to tell her," Bill says.

"Me, too," Bertha says. "Poor Willie."

"And she thanked him," Carl says. "Can you believe it? She thanked him."

"They say that's the kind of person she is." Bill reaches for Carl's cigarettes. "Always thinking of somebody else."

"Well, I hope Willie gets some rest now," Bertha says. "He looked so drug out I felt sorry for him."

"A thing like that's bound to work on a fella," Carl says. "You just never expect it in a man Joe's age."

"Still, it was better Willie finding him than her," Bertha says.

"Wouldn't that have been a fright?" Carl says.

"Can you imagine," she says, "walking in and seeing him there?"

"With his hand stretched out toward your picture and all?" Carl shakes his head. "That really got to me."

"I'll bet it was the last thing he did, too," Bertha says. "Sort of gives you a warm feeling to think about it."

Bill hunches his shoulders. "Gives me the goddamn creeps."

"I wonder what was going through his mind?" Carl says.

Bertha sighs. "Some say your whole life flashes by."

"That's when you drown," Bill says, blowing a stream of smoke toward the ceiling.

"He'd have a lot to think about," Carl says. "As much as he had going on."

"Nobody could claim he wasted any time, that's for sure," Bertha says. "But I guess none of it makes much difference now."

"Nope." The metal ashtray pings as Bill taps it with his cigarette. "When you're dead, you're dead."

The towel wrapped around her finger, Bertha rubs a brown spot on the counter. Her head is down, her voice husky. "It don't seem fair sometimes. Why does it always have to be the good ones?"

Carl turns to peer out the window, lifting his cap and setting it back in place. "What was it old Willie said? 'That's the way things are,' wasn't it? 'Like this snow. It just happens.'"

Beside Still Waters

On that day the river ran deep, small swirls pitting the surface. The water had the consistency of cream and the rich grey-brown color of the earth. Cottonwoods and elms and sycamores laid down humid dark shadows where gnats swarmed in lacy bunches and dragonflies hovered first one place, then another. The breeze had died an hour before, leaving behind the smell of catfish and carp.

His thumb rested lightly on the line that stretched through the eyes of the rod to a quiet pool near the opposite bank. The line bowed slightly from its own weight, water drops glistening along it like glass beads. His thumb rose from the reel, resettled, and he turned his head slowly in my direction.

I looked down at my tackle. The base of my rod was secured under a stone, its middle supported on a sturdy y-shaped limb he had carved and stuck into the clay. I was to leave it alone until I got a bite. He did not want me casting here and there, tangling our lines, or worse losing a hook and sinker on a submerged log.

In those years he seldom took me to the river. We went instead to Doyle Creek where we caught bullheads and perch and an occasional bass not big enough to keep. It did not matter, since no serious fishing was intended.

On the river it was different. There was no running up and down the bank, no tossing of pebbles or sticks into the water. There was no idle talk. The river was not a place for children.

He whipped his rod upright. The line pulled taut, slackened. He patiently reeled in, the rod wiggling as the bait and sinker bucked the current. He leaned the rod over his left leg and studied the wad of doughball on the hook. He squeezed it in his fist. It hung like a small pear from the end of the line. He cast again into the same spot, then sent me to the tent.

If it had been for something else, I would not have cared. I would have enjoyed the climb through tall grass and prickly weeds into the fresher air above the bank. I would have gotten a drink for myself and maybe a Hershey bar. I would have sat for a while listening to the birds in the trees and the far away sound of trucks on the highway. I would have felt good and wished the fishing trip could have been a week long instead of overnight.

The tent was on a patch of raised ground between two giant elm trees. Even though it was well-shaded, and the front flap and rear window were open, the air inside was hot and smelled of baked canvas. Our gear was stacked in orderly piles at the foot of the cots so we would know where things were in the dark. I untied his duffel bag and found the rubber boots. There was a pint of gin in each. One was usually enough, but he always brought the second because you just never knew.

I ate a plain Hershey bar, then another with almonds, breaking each into squares which I let melt on my tongue. I did not want to go back. If I did, he would start drinking and I would have to ask him before he drank too much. They all thought he was going to hell, my mother included, because he had not been baptized. I was supposed to talk him into it. I was his favorite grandson and he would listen to me, they said. If he died unsaved, it would be my fault.

He remained motionless as I slid down the bank behind him. His leathery neck was wet with sweat, but he did not loosen the collar of his long-sleeved shirt, nor take off the tight-fitting felt hat that creased his hair. That was how you stayed cool, he said. Not by undressing. He knew from thirty years under the sun, laying railroad track, repairing track.

He reached toward me without looking. The little finger and ring finger of each hand were drawn permanently to his palm, his thumb and first two fingers working like pincers as he held the bottle and unscrewed the cap.

Little bubbles rode up the glass. His shoulders jerked back, then he slouched forward and gasped. He raised the bottle a second time. When he had finished, the pint was half empty.

His eyes were already bleary as he pushed the bottle at me, asking gruffly if I wanted some, but not expecting me to take it. He would have been hurt and disappointed if I had.

"You better check your bait," he said.

My rod arched, the line slicing the murky water as I reeled it in. There was no fight, no running with the current. Only a steady, even drag.

"Goddamn turtle," he said. It floated a foot off the bank, neck craning, mouth working against the embedded hook. "Now keep that line tight." He inched his way down to cut the turtle loose. Slipping on the gumbo, he caught himself, one hand clutching a clump of bluegrass as he swiped at the line with his pocketknife.

Someone else would have walked straight to the water's edge, severed the line and been done with it. But at seventy, he still could not swim. He refused to get into a boat and once hiked the entire shoreline of the county lake—some five miles—rather than row across it with my father. He would not even put on a pair of waders, much less use them. His fear of water was complete.

The mere thought, then, of walking unprotected into a baptistery and letting someone dunk him "like a damn doughnut" was terrifying, and he told our minister so. Reverend Morton suggested he trust in God. My grandfather said it would be better not to get into a situation where your life depended on trusting anybody.

The turtle was free. It slid backwards, out of sight, a ripple on the water where its head had been.

I tied a on a new hook and sinker and rebaited with a fresh piece of chicken liver. He told me to try down where a cottonwood tree leaned out over the river. I cast just short and let the line flow into place.

He opened the gin bottle, took a drink and set it aside.

"Storm's coming," he said, making the obligatory comment on the weather that preceded any serious discussion. "You can feel it, can't you? By nightfall the air'll be so heavy you won't be able to breathe and all hell'll break loose. Blow? Yes, sir, it's going to blow."

He gazed at me, hazel eyes glittering for a moment, then turned back to his fishing line.

"You know your grandma's dying."

I nodded. Each time I visited, another piece of her seemed to be missing. She had never had toes, as far as I knew. Then her feet were gone, then her legs to her knees, then half her thighs. Gangrene from too much sugar in her blood.

"I hate it," he said. "I hate it like everything. She's been a good old pal." He stared at the folds the current left in the water. "I don't know what I'll do without her."

"Maybe you won't have to," I said.

"No, boy, there's no sense trying to fool ourselves."

"I don't mean that way."

"Oh," he said. "The other. The one where you get right with God or Jesus or whoever and everybody walks together in Glory. That what you mean?"

"Yes."

"Except getting right isn't right until you're baptized. Is it, now?"

I shook my head.

"That's what I figured."

"There's really nothing to it," I said, scooting closer, wanting to tell him how easily I had walked into the baptistery and let Reverend Morton put the handkerchief over my face and lower me backwards into the water in the name of the Father and the Son and the Holy Ghost.

"Then why do it?" he said, eyes narrowing.

"So you can be saved."

"For what, boy? From what?"

He hunched over his gin bottle and I reeled in a couple feet of line.

"Hell, nobody wants to die," he said. "But it's going to happen. You understand me? That much won't change, no matter what."

We were silent for some time. I was trying to imagine my grandmother walking with God, even with no legs. Then I wondered if she really could feel the missing parts and what they had done with them once they had cut them off. Had they ground them into dog food the way they did with horses? She was sitting at the living room window, curtains parted with one hand, eyes fixed on the hole in the hedge where neighborhood kids slithered through and tore off around the garage. Her hand came away, so perfectly white, and swept down to collect her sewing. But it was not in the place she thought it was. Instead, it was there where her lap dropped suddenly away over the ends of stumps, skin stretched around and stuffed up inside like bread dough. She arched her back and twisted in her wheelchair, as though caught by a sudden spasm of pain. When she opened her eyes again, she saw me at the doorway and knew I had witnessed the whole thing, and she held out her hand and asked if I wanted a cookie. I ran out the door through the hedge and up the street until my chest burned and my legs buckled.

"Good God, boy, take it! Take it!"

The line sang off my reel. I snapped the rod back. The hook set. The fish dove, plunging to the deepest reaches of the river, and I was with him, down to where my ears hurt and my breath was forced from me.

"Don't let him have too much." He was beside me, the smell of gin coating the hot air. "Take up the slack. That's it. Let him have a little now. Good. Work him. Tire him out. That's our supper, boy. That's our supper you've got there."

I heaved on the rod, hoping the line would break.

"No, Goddamnit!" But he did not stop me. He did not take the rod and reel from me. He backed away with a single bob of his head and let me go on with it.

I brought in the fish, a large channel cat. It had slick grey skin, fat dangling whiskers at the corners of its mouth, a dirty white, nearly yellow belly. Its gills gaped and closed like bellows. I put two fingers in the left gill slit to hold him and located the hook deep at the back of his throat.

"Leave it," he said. "We'll get it when we clean him."

I cut the line and passed the stringer through the gill where my fingers were. I let the fish gently down into the water and he hugged the mud bottom, motionless, while I anchored the stringer to a tree root.

"I guess we know now who the fisherman is in this family. Don't we?" He reached out to touch me, to tousle my hair as he always did.

I looked away.

His arm dropped and he returned to the bare spot hollowed out between knots of grass, where he picked up his bottle, eyed the line stretching from his rod and reel to the quiet pool near the opposite bank and sat back down to fish.

An Arrangement of Pieces

We are there, all of us gathered around like figures in an old family photograph, women seated in front, hats squared, purses clasped in laps, men behind, collars half-closed with narrow ties, and all of us fading brown and grey in the heat of a Kansas summer.

The hired preacher from Garnett lowers his pale head, intoning ashes to ashes, dust to dust, and prays over the bronze-finished coffin of our dearly beloved husband, father, son and friend who has passed from this earth. Ah-men, nose and chin nearly touching in solemnity.

Wind snaps the fringes of the green canvas canopy over the grave. The rope on a flagpole clangs. Our mother weeps silently, folded shut on her chair in front of the coffin. Our sister touches but does not hold her. Other women cry, too. Men look down, swallowing, not knowing what to do with burly-knuckled hands crossed before them.

The wind surges, retreats. The flag crackles like a log on fire.

The undertaker nods that we should leave, but no one moves. He starts toward our mother, arm outstretched. She waves him away. He comes closer, saying her name, reaching for her elbow. It's over now, it's time to go. Again, then again. She rises, frail and unsteady, each step a thought, heel and toe, heel and toe, and the wind catches her, pressing her dress to her body, sailing her between son and daughter toward the waiting car. The gust dies. She pats her son's hand to stop. Dry grass splinters under their feet as they turn to look back.

For a moment everything is still—the canopy, the coffin, the two gravediggers, the undertaker—breathlessly still, like props set against the white-hot summer sky, and the scene burns its image on our brains.

As if cued by the undertaker, a flock of starlings swoops down on a nearby field, the canopy ripples in the wind, a gravedigger taps a clod of dirt with his toe. She releases a sigh, and with a twitch of the fingers in her husband's direction, gets into the car.

II

He was born here. Here he grew to manhood. Here he is buried, beside his father. We creep through the streets block by block, gravel splattering the fenders of our car. Colony is a small town, where people live in houses with yards bald from age. What grass there is sprouts in the crumbling curbs on Main Street, in brick sidewalks, around stumps of trees, like hair from an old man's ears. There is no longer the sound of children playing. Of those who still live here, many are family—his aunts, uncles, cousins—and they have gathered at the church to receive us.

"FIRST COMMUNITY CONGREGATION" the glass-covered billboard by the sidewalk announces in white stick-on letters. Set well back from the street is a narrow frame building, an arched stained-glass window in front, opaque from the outside. Above it the steeple rises white on white into the sky. Up a flight of tilted cement steps a door stands open to the dark interior. We climb toward it, hand after hand along the peeling steel pipe rail.

The foyer smells of damp church bulletins, the grass welcome mat, old air that clings to the walls like flies. Near the entrance to the sanctuary, a stairwell descends to a white door, slightly ajar. Cool basement air brings with it a babble of voices.

Speckled brown tiles cover the floor of the fellowship hall, a single row of green around the perimeter. Three long tables jut toward us from the far end of the room, another perpendicular to them at the back wall where a lighted copy of Sallman's Head of Christ hangs. The tables are draped with white cloths, silverware and napkins set before black metal folding chairs.

People have collected in groups behind the two floor fans aimed at the tables. Those from town gather in the middle where they talk in low voices. Strangers sit or stand near the wall, saying nothing. The preacher from Garnett, himself an out of towner, perches on top of a cabinet, his Bible near his left hand, surveying the crowd. A man approaches him, nods toward us. The preacher hops to the floor, folding his Bible to his chest.

Our grandmother goes to him, shakes his hand, then begins introducing us to all those people whom we have heard about but have never met: Uncle Milt, Aunt Gertie, Uncle Claude, Aunt Emma, the Fairbanks sisters, a pair of third cousins. A few are left whose names even she has forgotten. Condolences and comments on how hot and dry it is, what a terrible time it is for something like this to happen.

The preacher prays that God bless the food to the use of our bodies, and a line forms, our mother and grandmother at the head. There are platters of ham, tuna and bologna sandwiches, cut on the diagonal, three trays of jello salad, a bowl of coleslaw, a bowl of potato chips, pies and cakes, and two sweating pitchers of tea that tastes like stale ice cubes.

After we are seated, discussions spring up on the way things are and were, prices and politics, life as usual. Our father's name is mentioned when a person telling a story about him wants a date to finish it, and someone provides the information with yet another story, which in turn needs clarifying. On and on until a portrait of him appears that is larger than any that has previously been drawn, for assembled here are people from every phase of his life, with different remembrances, stories, versions of him. They are all kind, depicting a man far more free and accomplished—happy—than was the case. It is, after all, a time for myth-making and not debunking and with her silence our mother acquiesces. The dark tones we will fill in later in private.

An hour passes, nearly two. We have consumed the coolness of the basement, and those who smoke escape back to the sun and wind. The rest sit, staring at smeared dessert plates, lapsing into comfortable habits and conversations. One of the fans has developed a trill that alternates in and out of hearing with the regularity of someone breathing in deep sleep. Women from the church come and go, clearing tables, putting food away. Done, they stand outside the kitchen door wiping their hands on flowered cotton aprons.

Our brother touches our grandmother's shoulder. Her head jerks up. She was only resting her eyes. We smile. Since we're staying over, she tells us, we'd best go on out to Gertie's before it gets too late. People look down, suddenly interested in spots on tablecloths. But they soon nod that they can see how anybody could be confused. It has been a stressful day, after all, and it's late and we still have such a drive ahead of us.

We begin taking our leave, thanking the church women for the lunch, the preacher from Garnett for coming, the relatives for their support and love. At the door there are hugs, kisses and handshakes and vows to do anything to help, anything at all.

And we wave goodbye again, saying things they cannot hear but which we know they will understand as we strap ourselves in for the long trip home.

III

We travel in two cars, our brother and sister, our mother and grandmother in one, spouses and an uncle and aunt in the other. After coming to open road, we play cat and mouse, passing each other, honking, booing, making faces, like high schoolers on a fieldtrip. As our mother turns to watch the rush of dry ditch weeds and pavement out the side window and our grandmother again closes her eyes, the steady tug of the road, the sound of motors, and the suck of the wind combines with them to bring us back to order as we drive on.

The highway loops up and down hills, mile after mile without a curve. Gullies crease the land, some tufted with scrub oak and bramble bushes, others bare wrinkles beside limestone outcroppings. Small ponds and water tanks dot the bottoms of valleys like shiny metal buttons fastening the weathered cloak of grass to the earth. Cattle graze with the sun, following trails in the flinty soil that thread away from the water and back again. It is a vast, awesome place, beautiful and terrifying in its emptiness.

A cattle truck peaks the hill ahead of us, gradually gaining momentum in its descent, trailer rocking, smoke puffing from the exhaust pipe as the driver runs through the gears. Like a roller coaster gone mad it crashes past us, metal clanging, tires singing, a flash of fur between slatted boards, in its wake the odor of hot rubber and manure. As the bad air clears, there are remarks about speed, the condition the meat will be in when it reaches the stockyards, the foolishness of pushing that hard for anything, since in the end nothing much matters.

In the gathering dusk, there seems to be little left to say. Our brother switches on the radio. It spits static at him. He slams the dash with his fist and curses. Our mother glances up, raising her hand as if to stroke the back of his head the way she used to to soothe our father. Her face pales, hand dropping to her purse for a cigarette.

And the land falls slowly away, valleys becoming more shallow, hills more rounded. Hedgerows give shape to fields of wheat and corn. Farmhouses, barns, silos stand out against the brilliant reds and golds of sunset. We pass the last slim ridge of hills, gliding as if onto the beach of an endless ocean. Our headlights pick up nothing but white lines on the road, grass and trees beside it, as darkness settles over the plains.

Publishing Credits

Some of the works in this collection have appeared in slightly different form in the following publications:

"Camille" in THE WILLIAM AND MARY REVIEW;

"Going Home" in LITTLE BALKANS REVIEW;

"The Auction" in QUARTET;

"Falling Out" in THE COTTONWOOD REVIEW;

"For Those Who Favor Fire" in AMELIA;

"Small Talk" in DESCANT;

"Winter Solstice" in VANDERBILT REVIEW;

"Habits Not Easily Broken" in WITNESS;

"The Man Who Wanted to Make Things Grow" in NIMROD;

"A Place Like Harry's" in GREEN'S MAGAZINE;

"The Unpredictability of Kansas Winters" in WIND;

"Beside Still Waters" in OUTERBRIDGE;

and "An Arrangement of Pieces" in THE LAUREL REVIEW.

About the Author

Gary D. Wilson is the author of the novels *Sing, Ronnie Blue* and *Getting Right*. Although his short fiction has appeared in numerous national literary magazines, *For Those Who Favor Fire* is his first published collection of stories. His work has been recommended for a Pushcart Prize, and he was a finalist for the Iowa Short Fiction Award and the Drue Heinz Literary Prize. He lives in Chicago.

Made in United States
North Haven, CT
30 July 2022

22043284R00109